PLAYING THE GAME

PLAYING THE GAME

A SPORTS NOVEL BY
DEL HARRIS
—WITH—
LOUIS AND KAY MOORE

WORD BOOKS
PUBLISHER
WACO, TEXAS

A DIVISION OF
WORD, INCORPORATED

PLAYING THE GAME

Library of Congress Cataloging in Publication Data

Harris, Del, 1937–
    Playing the game.

    Summary: Three teenaged boys learn to think positively and direct themselves toward goals, while experiencing the ups and downs of an exciting basketball season.
    [1. Basketball—Fiction.   2. Christian life—Fiction]
I. Moore, Louis.   II. Moore, Kay.   III. Title.
PZ7.H24124Pl 1984   [Fic]   84–11808
ISBN 0–8499–2967–9

Printed in the United States of America

I have fought the good fight,
I have finished the race,
I have kept the faith.
2 Timothy 4:7, RSV

Contents

PLAYING THE GAME

1

Hitting the Bottom

Billy Williams prodded a stray piece of popcorn with the toe of his sneaker and then angrily pulverized it into the floor of the basketball court until the kernel became nothing more than a small mound of white flakes.

The popcorn, along with an assortment of peanut hulls and potato-chip crumbs, had rained from the stands minutes earlier when someone from the Trimble High bleachers protested the team's embarrassing performance that evening.

Billy could hardly blame the fans for being miffed. For four straight games now, the Trimble team had performed like a bevy of first-graders, floundering around the court in disarray as their opponents outmaneuvered them on the scoreboard.

It was bad enough that Trimble, the defending all-district champs, fell last week to Morristown, a team from the next county which finished in the district cellar last season and was regarded as a lightweight in basketball circles.

But to be whipped tonight by North Side, which had only two lettermen returning from last year's squad and was winless for the current season so far! Billy imagined the scornful looks he would get in the school hallways tomorrow and wondered how he could fake illness if tonight's game ended in a loss.

Actually, Billy already found himself getting a sick headache as he listened to the annoying rumble from the opposite bleachers, while the North Side fans blared, "Make the Tigers Trimb-ble, Trimb-ble. Make the Tigers Trimb-ble, Trimb-ble." And from the looks on the faces of the hometown fans, Billy was not the only person not feeling well. In this small Indiana town of 20,000, basketball was king, and fans of all ages took any loss as a serious infraction.

Coach Ramsbottom had lectured the team on this subject in a pre-game conference, when the players, already demoralized because of their last three losses, gathered before the opening buzzer sounded.

"Don't you bums forget for one minute what counts in the town of Trimble," he bellowed in his loudest drill-sergeant tones, which players during his twenty-five years of coaching had come to recognize as more bark than bite. "It ain't oil wells; it ain't banks. It ain't pretty houses with white picket fences. It's basketball. With a capital *B*. The people who live here will string you jokers up by your toenails if you give them a bummer season. Now get out there and play like you're in high school instead of grammar school."

But the team was obviously doing anything but following his advice.

This whole evening might have turned out differently had it not been for Clark Symons, Billy concluded—as he found himself almost rooting for North Side out of his anger and shame.

Any number of times tonight Billy felt that he had been wide open for some easy lay-ups that could have piled more points on the Tigers' 30–27 half-time lead. But Billy felt that Clark wanted to monopolize the limelight and get himself named Most Valuable Player again. Tonight, in Billy's estimation, Clark had hogged the ball and missed some obvious points, putting the Tigers badly behind midway in the fourth quarter. From then on, the Tigers lost momentum which they could not seem to recover—and now there was only 5:22 left in the game.

Clark was Billy's biggest rival on the team. The two had battled this year for point production and had never been able to get along personally as a result. Billy regarded Clark as a Johnny-come-lately who took up basketball late in the summer when he failed to make the Trimble varsity football team.

On the other hand, Billy had eaten, breathed, and slept basketball ever since a teacher installed a basketball goal on the school playground when Billy was in kindergarten. In fact, almost as soon as he was old enough to crumple a piece of paper into a ball shape, Billy had swaggered through his house tossing his makeshift "basketballs" into any imaginary goal in sight—over door facings, around shower-curtain rods, onto closet shelves.

This greatly dismayed his parents, who gave him a tongue-lashing any time they caught him involved in one of his paper tosses. In fact, it seemed to Billy that his parents were always giving him a tongue-lashing about one thing or another—the same way they now lectured him about spending too much time with his new girl friend, Sally Rankin.

Although he grew into a lean 6'4" teenager and began to excel in basketball, Billy felt he could never fully win the approval of his parents, even on the glory nights when he managed to best Clark and be the Tigers' high-scorer for the evening. In fact, one night when Billy scored twenty-four points and broke a school record, his parents were not even in the stands to see him recognized.

Despite his parents' seeming nonchalance about his basketball involvement, Billy loved the sport fervently. Perhaps that was why he was so angered when Coach Ramsbottom earlier tonight had removed Billy from the lineup and instructed team captain Freddie Malone to get the ball to Clark any time he found Clark open on the court.

Billy had suspected all year that the coach was growing partial to Clark, since the player's father recently bought the only sporting-goods store in Trimble and gave Ramsbottom a handsome discount on whatever school or personal items he needed. Lately, Ramsbottom always chose Clark over Billy in the tense situations, and Billy thought Ramsbottom's motive was thinly veiled.

Besides suspecting this minor conspiracy, Billy also felt that Freddie Malone was a culprit in this evening's disaster. He suspected that Freddie was beginning to side with Clark in this cozy arrangement simply to curry favor with Ramsbottom. For example, early after the opening tip of the game, Freddie had dribbled the ball to the middle, with Billy and Clark flanking him on either side on the fast break. Freddie drew the defense to his side and motioned toward Billy, who was wide open. But instead of following through, Freddie bounced a pass straight to Symons for the lay-up. It was a well-executed play, but Billy frowned to Freddie, "Hey, man, I was a shoo-in on that one." Freddie merely shrugged and made no comment.

In the second quarter, Freddie continued to toss the ball to Clark, who scored three more times in the first three minutes. Billy sidled up to Beck Beckwith and begged, "Beck, I'm playing in this game too, you know. Freddie is passing to Symons every time. How about getting us something going on our side of the floor?"

Beck had agreed, and the two tried to take the game into their own hands even though the Tigers led 24–16 at that point—merely on the strength of Clark's shooting. Billy forced two long shots which failed to connect, and Beck threw the ball out of bounds while trying to feed Billy on a back-door cut. North Side capitalized on their bumbling and tied the game 24–24.

The antics of Billy and Beck had cost Trimble the lead. Ramsbottom stormed over, jerked Billy out and benched him for trying to steal the show. With Billy gone, Clark was free to put on some additional scoring theatrics, and the Tigers took their 30–27 lead into the locker room.

However, Ramsbottom was still fuming and shouted, "What is the matter with you dilberts out there that you can't play together? We get going pretty good and then someone grows afraid that he isn't getting his share of the glory. When that happens, our game goes straight down the pipe. Don't you know that when we stay together we can all go to the party, but if we try it alone, none of us gets an invite? Now you bums better come through this time. No more of that selfish stuff." Glaring at Billy as he spoke, he refused to start him when the second half began.

When the North Side coach realized at the start of the third quarter that Billy was still not in the lineup, he switched his defense back to man-to-man instead of the zone in the first half that was deliberately engineered with Billy in mind. Clark and his two subordinates, Joe Wilson and Bobby Prentice, were not as effective against the man-to-man defense as they had been against the previous arrangement. Within four minutes in the third quarter, the Tigers had fallen behind 38–34.

Deciding that Billy had been punished enough, Ramsbottom nodded him back in for a second chance.

Determined to show the coach that he was invaluable to the team, Billy immediately amassed seven rebounds—four on the offensive board and three conversions into rebounding baskets. He showed spunk on defense by stopping his opponent cold, and he managed two driving lay-ups and two jumpers from the side.

At the third-quarter stop, the count was 49–43 in favor of Trimble. Billy had scored fourteen points. He entered the fourth-quarter huddle feeling smug and secure and murmured to Beck, "Now the old buzzard will see who's boss of this team."

Clark, who had sat out the third stanza while Bobby Prentice was in, had been doing some brooding on his own during his stint on the bench. Instantly now, with Clark back on the court, the battle began afresh between Clark and Billy, and the two immediately scrambled again for leadership on the court instead of forging ahead so that Trimble could put the game out of reach. While Trimble dallied in getting its act together, North Side ran off four straight field goals to take a 53–49 lead with 5:22 on the clock.

"Williams, you jerk, get off the court and don't go back," Ramsbottom screeched within full earshot of many of the fans, who laughed aloud at his display.

Billy, stomping off the floor, grabbed the warm-up jacket that someone handed him and threw it tempestuously on the bench as he sat down, stuffing his face into a towel.

As Billy reflected bitterly over what had gone wrong, and as the chips and popcorn poured from the stands in protest, the game ended with North Side 64, Trimble 52. Incredibly, Trimble had lost the game after leading by six points at the end of the third quarter.

As the crowd of Trimble faithfuls began filing dejectedly from the stands, Billy lifted his eyes from his towel long enough to catch a glimpse of his girl friend Sally, who was captain of the cheerleading squad. Sally managed a weak smile as she led a few remaining fans in singing the Trimble Alma Mater.

As the song reached the line that said, "To our players bold, we raise the blue and gold," Sally looked over at Billy and gave him a meek thumbs-up sign. The gesture brought a moment of cheer to Billy, because it was a reminder that at least he still had Sally, clearly the most popular girl at Trimble and a coveted catch by any standards.

Two months before, when Sally had agreed to go with Billy

to the Homecoming Dance on their first date, Billy sped to basketball practice that day so he could boast to his teammates, many of whom Sally had turned down for dates in the past. Now Beck Beckwith, who had witnessed Sally's signal to Billy just then, spoiled Billy's reverie by snarling, "If you think she'll still be seen with you after a loser of a game like tonight, you're nuts."

Billy was uncomfortably aware that the blonde cheerleader had never given him a second glance until the *Trimble Town Sentinel* last fall had pegged Billy to be the driving force behind the Tiger team this season.

Beck suspected that Sally was the kind of girl who dated whoever happened to be the athletic kingpin at the moment. He sensed that her ardor would cool if Billy had many more unsuccessful evenings like tonight.

The post-game locker-room scene was predictably tense. The room was divided into three angry clusters, with shouts and insults being exchanged in a giant verbal free-for-all. "Some people want to score all the points on this team," came the cry from one section of the room. Another section bit back, "Some people couldn't score if they were left alone in the gym for an hour."

The bickering quieted only when Ramsbottom lifted his military tones over the din. "As far as I'm concerned, each of you is just as bad as the next guy. You just rolled over in the last quarter. You'd play with spirit for two or three minutes, then decide it's time to knock off for the day. I think it's time you decide whether you want to be ballplayers or not. I might as well call up the rest of the teams on our schedule for the season and tell them we forfeit—because you players don't care."

The players, who normally wrote off Ramsbottom's bombastic post-game lectures, were unusually hushed after his latest remarks.

Billy perceived that the monologue was finished, as Ramsbottom paced up and down the locker room for several seconds. Eager to flee the scene, Billy started to undress. But Ramsbottom was not ready for anyone to jump the gun.

"Symons, did I say it was time for anyone to change clothes?" Ramsbottom demanded, in a shot clearly aimed at Billy.

"No sir," responded Clark, surpressing a snicker at his rival's misdeed.

"What is it, Williams? Got someplace to go, do you? Oh, well, what's one more lost game to you anyway? You scored lots of points tonight. That's all you suit up for, isn't it?"

With that, the coach stormed out the door, leaving the players standing in uncomfortable silence. Flushed and miserable, Billy raced to finish dressing without a word to anyone. The coach had deserted the players, leaving them to ponder the game alone without his guidance. And after Beck's remarks earlier, Billy now wondered if Sally would desert him, too.

To his relief, Sally was waiting by the Coke machine in the half-darkened gym. Billy felt a little smug when he saw her. Although the hour was late and it was a school night, Billy felt like going for a long drive in the country.

Sure, his parents would yell again, just as they had made a federal case after every other game when he took Sally for a drive. But Billy decided that after an evening like this one, he might as well separate Ramsbottom's humiliating diatribe and his folks' predictable explosion with a small romantic interlude.

2

A Mixed Bag of Worries

Fred Ramsbottom, coach of this evening's luckless Tigers, settled his considerable bulk into the windowed booth at Shipley's All-Nite Grill. This lackluster diner had for years been the coach's after-game place of escape, where he could sit and ponder whatever match had just concluded.

Shipley's was located seven miles outside of town along a busy interstate. Ramsbottom had chosen this as his unwinding spot because he could blend in anonymously with the truck drivers while he let the evening's events pass in review on the screen of his mind.

Tonight, as he sat by his usual window and watched the trucks streak along the highway, Ramsbottom was so despondent that he was halfway tempted to stand by the road and hitch a ride going somewhere—anywhere that would take him far away from basketball and Trimble.

Almost instantly, however, guilt waves washed over Ramsbottom for having such disloyal thoughts. Twenty-five years ago, Trimble had taken him in as an idealistic youth who had just graduated from college and was eager to coach. How could he ever walk out on a town that had coddled him with every conceivable honor during his years at the coaching helm?

In the ensuing years, Ramsbottom had become as much of an institution in Trimble as was the statue of Judge Hatton V. Trimble which stood in front of the courthouse. In fact, local citizens sometimes wondered if they would someday drive past the courthouse to see that the judge's bronzed form had been replaced by a statue of Ramsbottom.

Last year, as on the many other occasions when Trimble had taken the all-district crown, a rash of "Ramsbottom for Mayor" bumper stickers appeared around town. The slogans were circulated half in jest, half in earnest, as the coach rode the crest of the team's success.

As Trimble had developed into a basketball powerhouse, Ramsbottom had been named Citizen of the Year by the Trimble newspaper more often than anyone could remember. Moreover, when the school board unanimously voted to name the sparkling new basketball arena "Fred Ramsbottom Field," no one dared utter a word of protest.

However, the fact that Trimble, Indiana, was consumed by basketball made Ramsbottom wonder—on this evening when his team had suffered its fifth straight loss—just exactly how forgiving the town would be if this downward slump continued.

Ramsbottom knew that the same fans who took up a collection to buy him a custom-made blue-and-gold Chevy last spring, in honor of his twenty-fifth anniversary at the school, could just as quickly be after his neck if something did not happen soon to snap the Tigers' losing streak.

In fact, last week after Trimble's embarrassing loss to Morristown, Ramsbottom noticed that several cars on the student parking lot were sporting new bumper stickers. Instead of reading "Ramsbottom for Mayor," these new ones said, "Has Ramsbottom Bottomed Out?"

Just last night, on the eve of the North Side game, there

had been a mysterious telephone call to his home, with a husky male voice that said, "Ramsbottom, you're a has-been. Better start packing."

Suddenly, job security, which had never particularly troubled Ramsbottom before, began keeping the coach awake at night. Where would a forty-five-year-old coach who was passionately devoted to his town and his team look for work if the people here suddenly turned against him?

It was not as if this was Trimble's first losing season in its history. The last time, four years ago, Trimble finished in the district cellar after winning only three starts during its four-month season. Three years before that, Trimble fell apart in the last part of the season, after being undefeated in its first seven games. But on those occasions, there had always seemed to be some good excuse, some easy alibi that the sports columnists could use to explain away the unfortunate turn of events.

For example, the scion of Indiana sports columnists, Wade Rafferty, had written that Trimble's last-place finish four years ago was "easily due to the loss of star Jimmy Hawthorne because he broke his ankle in a motorcycle accident early in the year.

"We can only hope that Trimble will adopt the attitude of 'You can't win 'em all,' and that Coach Ramsbottom will know he still wins the Trimble popularity contest, win or lose on the court," the columnist had gushed at the end of the season.

During previous bummer times, the critics had always come up with some handle, such as bad refereeing or a new and more complex conference schedule, to help them write off any slipups. As usual, the beloved Coach Ramsbottom was let off the hook without a trace of blame.

But this year, Ramsbottom had sat up nights wracking his brain for some clue as to why the Tigers seemed bent on defeat at every turn. With more than half the team returning from last season's all-district squad, Ramsbottom had felt that his current players had more potential than had any group he had coached in recent memory. There had even been a spark of that potential tonight when Billy Williams turned in the splendid third-quarter performance that put Trimble ahead 49–43 as the Tigers entered the final period. There was no reason why that momentum could not have lasted for the rest of the game.

Two minutes later, though, it was as if a totally different herd of boys had emerged from the fourth-quarter huddle. In seconds, the Tigers seemed to be split into three warring camps with each of the three trying to grab all the marbles for its very own.

Suddenly it seemed that the Tigers were playing the Tigers, instead of concentrating all their energies on beating North Side. The selfishness that emerged ended up costing Trimble one of its most important games of the season.

Ramsbottom at first was willing to heap all the blame for the team's attitude on himself. Maybe last night's mystery caller was on target—maybe the coach *was* a has-been. Always in the past, Ramsbottom, who at 6′4″ was a giant hulk of a man, was able to use his staff-sergeant demeanor and sarcastic, negative psychology to arouse his players to action. His wry humor had always been well received by the team, as well as by the fans.

For example, last year toward the end of a game, he had chosen a quiet moment, during a free throw, to yell out to one of the players, "Hey, Burns, whatever you do, don't get your hair messed up out there." Everyone in the stands had howled, and such play-to-the-galleries antics had earned him the name of "Theatrical Fred." Some fans were drawn to the weekly games just to see Ramsbottom's performance.

But this year, instead of laughing at Ramsbottom's buffoonery, the team members seemed to bristle when Ramsbottom yelled out at them during games—which bothered him, since he never meant to offend and actually felt rather paternalistic about all of them.

His pre-game lectures, featuring his sarcastic wit, now seemed to have about as much effect as would pouring water on a yellow vinyl rainslicker. The boys now took him as seriously as they did a fly on the wall, which showed in their uninspired performance on the court.

However, even in his most desolate moments, Ramsbottom was not willing to shoulder all the blame. He had never before coached a squad that had so little concept of teamwork and whose players seemed so generally turned off with life in general.

Take Billy Williams, for example. Not only did Billy seem totally unfazed by the problems, but Ramsbottom could not even get Billy's father interested in the fate of the team, or in how his son was doing. One day when he bumped into Mr. Williams as the two waited in the drugstore for prescriptions to be filled, Ramsbottom tried to tell Billy's father how disappointed he was in the team this year and how he hoped to enlist the man's help.

"Personally, I just try not to get involved in these matters," said the elder Williams in a tone that Ramsbottom thought sounded haughty. "Billy spends far too much time on sports anyway, and it's high time he was finding out how meaningless it all is."

So Billy, desperate for his father's love and approval, continued in his efforts for attention, which he accomplished in ways that were not always constructive. Although he was a good basketball player, possibly the best on the team this year, he constantly annoyed his friends by boasting to the point of being obnoxious when he achieved the slightest accomplishment.

Ironically, for Billy himself, no accomplishment was ever enough. If he got all A's in a subject, Billy berated himself for not making all A+'s. If he scored twenty points in a game, he moped for days about not scoring thirty, believing that would surely be the key to gaining his parents' notice. Unfortunately, his outlandish bragging, which was an obvious cover-up for his poor self-esteem, got on others' nerves to the point that they wished Billy wore a muzzle.

On the other hand, group acceptance was easy for Freddie Malone, who was less talented than Billy but had the leadership skills to get himself named captain of the basketball team. Freddie had the knack of finishing first in just about everything that he attempted, whether or not he had the actual ability. When it came time to promote an activity such as a candy sale or a paper drive, Freddie could get the class to rally behind the project—just by making one speech over the loudspeaker.

However, Freddie's popularity often led him to promote pranks as well. For example, in Spanish class one day, Freddie drove nervous Mrs. Hanna almost to tears by getting everyone in the room to make barn noises and insect chirps while the frazzled teacher was trying to talk. Ramsbottom felt that the team would be headed for the district crown at this very minute if Freddie could just channel his leadership skills into that direction instead of looking for mischief to stir up.

A far more amiable sort was a third player, Beck Beckwith, who did take the team seriously, probably because it was the only aspect of his life that money could not buy. As one might gather from the officious sound of Beck's formal name—Sheldon Mercer Beckwith—the family was well fixed. His father was vice-president and general manager of the StarCo Plastics Company, the town's biggest industry. Like Billy, Beck fought for his father's attention but for a different reason. Instead of being indifferent, as Mr. Williams was, Gordon Beckwith was just always away—either jetting to some remote spot on the globe or hunting game or playing golf. Beck's mother lived the expected role of the society wife and was usually playing tennis or attending charity meetings. She had probably seen Beck play basketball but once in his entire high-school career.

"Come on over to Beckwith's; his toys will make us all stars," was the team's credo, and deservedly so. The Beckwith mansion had a giant basketball court in the back yard, with lights for night play, and had a workout room in the upstairs guest quarters that would make some fitness centers look like dumps. There also was an Olympic-sized swimming pool and a wide variety of indoor games such as table tennis and billiards.

Needless to say, his house was the most popular hangout in town, for the local kids as well as some boys not from Trimble, whom Ramsbottom occasionally saw leaving basketball practice with Beck and his friends. Ramsbottom had once even questioned Beckwith about those extras, who seemed older than the other boys and somehow coarser and of a different caliber.

"They're just some guys I know from Morristown," Beck shrugged one day when Ramsbottom pressed him for details. "There's nothing to do where they live, so they come over here in the afternoons for a little fun."

Ramsbottom worried about the outsiders a little. But this worry was totally eclipsed by his greater concern about Beck himself, who was so eager to blend into the group and to avoid calling attention to himself and his money that he held back in his performance on the court. He did everything he could to keep a low profile, yet he was actually capable of giving 220 percent. Therefore, his basketball skills were always lurking beneath the surface, as though Beck were afraid to let anyone know his true abilities.

Perhaps his stable home life, with average but hard-working parents who took lots of interest in school concerns, was the reason Ramsbottom was partial to Clark Symons, tonight's high scorer and Billy William's archrival. Symons was an even-tempered youth who was seen by the other team members as a goody-goody and too squeaky clean to be of any use to them. Because his dad owned the sporting-goods store where Ramsbottom bought supplies, the coach often found himself visiting with Gene Symons on the day after a game. Clark's father was a good listener and a good sounding board for Ramsbottom, who was desperate for someone to commiserate with on a day like tomorrow would be after tonight's loss to North Side.

Ramsbottom knew that even this alliance had its troubles. In any post-game analysis, Gene Symons could hardly be objective about his son's role in the team snafus. What's more, his frequent visits at Symons' Sporting Goods had already caused tongues to wag that Ramsbottom favored young Symons on the court in order to get jerseys and sneakers for the team at a cut rate.

These were the items in Ramsbottom's bag of worries as he left Shipley's All-Nite Grill and drove back into town, where he most surely would take his lumps tomorrow.

As he rounded the last bend in the road and saw the lights and spires of the familiar town stretched out before him, Ramsbottom wanted to believe that the answer to the Tigers' problem lay out there somewhere behind one of those porch lights or under one of those roofs.

But finding his way through the challenge seemed to require almost more patience than one weary coach could muster.

3

A New Face in the Crowd

Among the spectators at Trimble's humiliating loss that evening to North Side was John Dyer, the new minister in town, who by now was growing used to seeing the Tigers head for the showers with egg on their faces.

A newcomer to Trimble from Indianapolis, Dyer had gone to the school's athletic office his first week in town to buy season tickets to the Tigers' games, since Trimble's reputation as a top-notch basketball power was widely circulated throughout the state.

At his first Trimble game last month, as he watched Billy Williams warm up on the sidelines and Freddie Malone bark directions on the floor, Dyer felt his heart pound in his chest just as it had during his own days on the college basketball team. With adrenaline suddenly flowing as forcefully as Niagara Falls, Dyer could close his eyes and picture himself standing at the free-throw line at that very moment, knowing that the fate of the game rose or fell on that one well-placed basketball.

Since graduating from Bering State University fifteen years

ago on a basketball scholarship, Dyer had been a spectator whenever he could find a game within a fifty-mile radius to attend. A recent widower with no family responsibilities, Dyer had looked forward to being one of the Tigers' most devoted spectators.

Before that first evening was over, Dyer began to wonder if he might not be better off spending evenings at the local bowling alley. The highly touted Trimble Tigers had put on a pathetic performance, not just during that miserable season opener, but for the next two games as well.

"I really feel for your Tigers this year," commiserated Dyer one day when he was first introduced to Ramsbottom at a Chamber of Commerce luncheon just before the Trimble-North Side game. "I'm sorry that the season isn't going better for you."

Ramsbottom managed a weak smile. "I know you ministers have connections in high places, but the way our boys are playing this year, I'm not sure even God himself could help us now."

The prospect of watching the Tigers play ball was one of the reasons Dyer had not minded when last summer he received his new pulpit assignment to be assistant minister in charge of youth at Union Church in small-town Trimble.

Besides, in the three years since his wife, Lucy, was killed in a traffic accident, Dyer had suddenly found big-city life too impersonal and haunting, with memories painfully etched on every street corner. Even though he had taken a significant cut in pay by moving to the smaller church in Trimble, he looked forward to being in a place where he could at last put the past behind him and where he could forge ahead with a new beginning.

Lulled by the more tolerant, anonymous atmosphere of Indianapolis, where people of all persuasions and lifestyles meshed into a larger melting pot, Dyer had not counted on the somewhat horrified stares he got from parishioners on the first Sunday he rode his motorcycle to services at Union

Church. His longish brown hair curled over the rim of his helmet, which was in stark contrast to the business suit he wore.

His church in Indianapolis had come to accept his cycle and his rather free-spirited approach to life as a part of him. Therefore, Dyer was startled when the chairman of the church board walked him to his motorcycle after services that morning and said to him quietly, "You know, this here's going to take some getting used to."

Dyer's motorcycle had always been the one outlet that he had refused to part with—even when Lucy had politely objected—because his bike had helped give him an entree to certain types of people who might not otherwise take church seriously.

In fact, it was Dyer's black Yamaha that broke the ice the first time the new minister met the Big Three of the Trimble basketball team—Freddie Malone, Beck Beckwith, and Billy Williams. The trio was gathered at their favorite after-school hangout, Hickle's Super Drugs. They went there daily to harass Alice Smoots, the humorless and vulnerable waitress who worked behind the soda counter and cringed whenever she saw the tall cagers walk into the drugstore every afternoon about this time.

Alice's plain face brightened in a great smile of relief when Dyer happened into Hickle's that afternoon to get a Coke float on his way home from church. She knew that this new visitor would mean a few moments' break from her tormenters.

"Ooooh, it's the new minister," she squealed in her most mouselike tones, as all eyes turned toward the helmeted figure approaching the counter. "Oh, Reverend, won't you sit down and make yourself comfy?"

The players turned from their shenanigans with Alice to eyeball Dyer's curious appearance. "You're a minister?" Billy finally managed in a shocked voice, "I mean, dressed like that? With a cycle and all?"

"Of course he is, you silly boys," Alice interjected, with

an instant air of superiority because she had already heard Dyer in church two Sundays ago and felt she finally had an edge over her daily detractors. "This is the new Reverend Dyer down at Union Church. You go there, don't you Billy? Or have you gotten so mean that they won't let you in now?"

Billy blushed a little at being put down by this mere slip of a waitress and mumbled, "I haven't been in a while." He suddenly recalled that Reverend Meth, the former assistant, had left several months ago and that the church had been looking all summer for a replacement.

Meanwhile, the other two boys were taking in every detail of Dyer's impressive Yamaha parked at the drugstore curb.

"Holy mackerel, what a beauty!" Beck admired, since a motorcycle was the one toy that even his rich father had refused to buy him, because Mr. Beckwith thought them too dangerous. "Is that really yours?"

"I just think of myself as a modern-day circuit rider," Dyer replied, with a mirthful twinkle in his blue eyes and a smile that was not the typical paste-on variety.

With that comment, the ice was formally broken, and the awestruck trio of boys scrambled back to their soda-fountain seats to introduce themselves rather awkwardly.

Actually, the boys were already known to Dyer, not just because they were wearing their pre-season basketball jerseys that afternoon, but because of their reputation at Union Church as incorrigible troublemakers.

Before he left for his new assignment, Meth gave Dyer a detailed briefing about the "state of the youth in the church." And the names of Beckwith, Malone, and Williams slipped into the conversation frequently as Meth outlined Dyer's problem areas as youth minister.

In truth, Meth blamed the boys' antics for the fact that he had not been very successful in winning conversions among the young people during his three years at Union Church.

"Every time I would get to some important Scripture, some message that I thought would put those youngsters under conviction, I would hear a noise that sounded like the low mooing of a cow," the exasperated Meth told Dyer on his first day at work. "Those three boys always wore suspicious looks, but what could I say? I didn't want to accuse anyone. But my lesson was always in shambles after that."

Beck and Freddie had started attending Sunday school about a year ago at Billy's insistence. Billy's parents were faithful Union members and made him come with them. Because the town of Trimble was a rather boring place on Sundays, Beck and Freddie decided it was worth the two tedious hours in church just to socialize a bit and to entertain their admiring school chums with basketball scuttlebutt.

However, as soon as the coffee-and-doughnut period was over and the boys had to settle down in their chairs and feign concentration, they became restless. Soon they were conspiring before class on how they could make a mockery of Reverend Meth's lesson. Making the animal noises—the same type of prank they played in school successfully with Mrs. Hanna— was actually Freddie's idea. Sitting in the back of the room, he sometimes began the low mooing, with the others chiming in. At other times, they interspersed the moos with assorted cat whines and insect chirps.

Since the leaders of this mischief were their adored town heros, the rest of Meth's class cheerfully went along with the gig, making it impossible for Meth to zero in on one particular culprit. In his frazzled view everyone in class looked equally guilty. So he merely tried to talk above the fracas, while the class members dissolved in giggles.

From what Dyer knew of Meth, however, he could hardly cast total blame on the boys for the unruly scenes that had developed among the youth group over the years. Meth's negative approach, that bordered on the antiquated "hellfire and damnation," made Dyer secretly wonder how the frustrated minister managed to hold an audience—young or old—for even five minutes.

Meth's talks were trite and unimaginative, illustrated with

outdated gimmicks such as flannelgraph stories of Jesus and the five loaves and two fishes that most of the youths remembered from their early grade-school Bible classes. The only way that Meth ever found to bring the teenage audience back from their separate worlds of thought was to yell in a loud, threatening voice such statements as, "Unless you want to be burned in eternal punishment, where there will be gnashing of teeth and tears forever, you'd better take this opportunity today to rid yourself of your sin: Take up the cross and follow Jesus."

With those bombastic words of warning from Meth, the class would quiet down for the first time that day—usually just in time for the dismissal bell.

Only once had Meth displayed an attempt at humor, which might have been his salvation with the young people if he had only cultivated that approach. One Sunday, when the mooing sounds and insect noises started, Meth startled everyone by responding casually, "I am glad to have all the various little creatures of God come to my classes, but I regret that the baptismal fount is not large enough to accommodate a cow."

With this smooth reaction and poised response, Meth caught the audience totally off guard. The trio of tormentors wondered among themselves if the pedantic Meth might be on the verge of becoming a pleasant person. Meth, stunned by the instant silence of the crowd, wondered if the boys might be on the verge of turning over a new leaf—maybe even on the verge of a conversion experience. Each party—Meth and the boys— left that day thinking they had scored points against the other.

Since old habits die hard, Meth was back the next Sunday, frazzled and serious as ever. So the noises continued. Shortly thereafter, Meth announced he was leaving Union to become senior minister in another city. To no one's surprise, his new job description did not include directing youth.

Upon Meth's resignation and with the summer coming on,

the youth department in Sunday school virtually disbanded. Beck went to Michigan to his parents' summer cottage for the three-month vacation. Billy, who had wheedled his chums into joining him at church in the first place, stayed home most of the summer because his mother was not feeling well after having back surgery—and there was no parental pressure to attend church. Freddie, who simply went along for the ride, certainly was not about to show up on his own. With Meth not around to harass, attending church held very little charm for any of the three.

Thus, when the boys had their chance meeting with John Dyer and his motorcycle at the drugstore in early September, it was the first time that church had entered their minds since summer began.

The group at the soda fountain made small talk for a while about the team and the upcoming season and Dyer's past connection with basketball. Then Billy asked, "You going to be like Reverend Meth and spend the whole time in church telling us how bad we are?"

"Well, Billy, I like to think of myself as a positive person," said Dyer, who by then had finished his Coke float and was paying Alice at the cash register. "I hope you'll find that I'm much more interested in building people up than cutting them down."

The boys stood mesmerized while Dyer revved up his motorcycle in front of Hickle's and headed toward home.

Beck broke the silence by wisecracking, "Boy, what a snowman! Somebody like that just can't be for real."

Billy chortled, "Real or not, I just wish a little of him would rub off on old man Ramsbottom. Our lives would sure be a lot happier this year if it did."

4

An Urgent S.O.S.

"Tigers' Poor Season Due to Faulty Teamwork, from Coach on Down!"

That was the gutsy headline that awaited Coach Ramsbottom when he arrived at school an hour early one morning, exactly a week after the loss to North Side.

In his first burst of enthusiasm since that depressing game, Ramsbottom had shown up at school before the students arrived, so he could reorganize some equipment before the day's crucial practice. Surely today would be the day, he thought, that the boys would finally get their acts together and start a fresh winning streak.

However, breezing past the teachers' lounge on his way to the gym, Ramsbottom's eyes fell on the banner headline of *The Tiger's Eye*, the Trimble school newspaper which lay in neatly folded stacks ready for students to pick up and devour just sixty minutes from now. Ramsbottom seized the paper and scanned the editorial quickly. Instantly forgetting about his original plans to work on equipment, he dashed back to his office to mull over the stinging words while no one was around to watch his blood boil.

"Never in the history of Trimble has the Tigers' basketball team been such an embarrassment to the student body," read the hard-hitting column, obviously the work of the newspaper's editor, Clay Rogers, whom Ramsbottom had long ago pegged as a smart aleck who never had a kind word on any subject.

"Keep in mind that this is the team that was picked to wear the district crown again this year. Keep in mind that this is the team that is the pride of Indiana. Keep in mind that this is a school where students are loyal to the core, packing the gym for every game and offering strong support, sometimes to the detriment of our classes and other school activities.

"The fault does not lie with the Trimble fans. What we see when we come to the games is a group of gold-jerseyed athletes who act like they are not even acquainted, much less members of the same basketball team. We see a coach who is so ineffective in rallying his team to action that one wonders if he is acquainted with these boys either.

"Perhaps someone from the student body should visit this afternoon's practice just so the players and coach can be introduced to one another. Unless some drastic action happens fast to bring the Tigers together for one purpose, the name of our team should by all rights be changed from the Trimble Tigers to the Trimble Turkeys.

"We feel we deserve something better."

Although hurtful, the editorial came as no actual surprise to Ramsbottom because it seemed to typify the way the Trimble students had responded during the past week, after the Tigers' fourth loss of the season.

The student body had been curt, sullen, and openly hostile in a way that Ramsbottom had never experienced. The antagonism was taking its toll on the players, who felt beaten down and had begun acting out their frustrations in the classroom and elsewhere

For example, in the Spanish class of Mrs. Hanna, the new teacher who had become the brunt of their occasional jokes, the boys stepped up their pranks. One day when Mrs. Hanna tarried too long in the principal's office before class, the boys under Freddie's leadership put the wastebasket on the outside ledge of the classroom's second-story window, in plain view of Mrs. Hanna when she walked in the door.

As the teacher walked over to her desk and bent down to get some papers from the bottom drawer, Freddie gave the signal and Billy threw a rubber ball against the wastebasket.

"Kawhop!" was the sound as ball met the green basket, which dived out the window. The ball bounced off the can and hit the front wall, caromed off a stand that suspended maps of the world, and then came to rest against Mrs. Hanna's foot.

The teacher was so shocked by the sudden crash that she sat down in her chair, where the impish students had rubbed chalk in thick dusty circles on the seat. She looked down in horror at the chalky residue that clung to the sides of her navy skirt.

To no one's surprise, she instantly exploded. "I have had enough of your stupid little games," she snapped. "You are the most immature group of high-school students I have ever seen. I will give you fifteen extra sentences to diagram for your homework tonight."

When they were not working on Mrs. Hanna, the boys were plotting tricks for Jump Otten, the unfortunate town wino always found leaning against the wall at the Night Owl Bar and Grill.

The trio considered Jump their own personal vaudeville act. By using a few well-rehearsed lines, they could set him off in the same predictable manner as a wind-up toy that repeats the same song whenever its key is turned.

Jump was very sensitive about his shaky legs that had been broken some years ago, on two different occasions, when he staggered in front of a passing car after a few drinks too many. As a result, he hated cars with a passion.

"Hey, Jump, how've the cars been treating you these days?" Freddie, the pranks chairman, yelled out as the boys spotted the wino in his familiar slouch against the tavern.

"Cars! I hate cars!" Jump responded as though by rote and sprang immediately into action, slapping his cane vehemently against the Nite Owl's window ledge.

At random, Freddie picked out some innocuous-looking car parked several feet away and pointed, "See that car over there? You recognize that car?"

Jump studied it, squinting his eyes as if trying to get some lost picture to focus in his mind. "No," he hesitated. "No, What about it?"

"That's the car that hit you the last time. What are you going to do about that?" asked Freddie, knowing exactly what Jump was going to do.

"Why, I'm going to beat the tar out of that car," Jump seethed, as he picked up his cane, moved with surprising swiftness to the vehicle, and gave it three hard whacks. Freddie, Billy, and Beck dissolved into hysterical laughter as they crept away from the scene.

For a grand finale to their show, Freddie ran back and gave Jump a slap across his backside, which caused that unfortunate to whirl around and leap four feet into the air in one of his sensational jumps, from which he got his nickname. However, before Jump could shake his finger at the initiator of the slap, Freddie had rejoined his teammates on the far side of the Nite Owl Grill, where the nearsighted Jump could no longer see them. They chortled over the day's conquest of Jump all the way home.

Besides such misdeeds, Ramsbottom was also concerned about Billy, who had already been late to three practices this week because he was off somewhere with Sally Rankin. Ramsbottom sensed that Billy, desperate to keep the popular coed's affections despite his declining hero status, had risked being in trouble with the coach rather than say no to Sally's demands on his time.

Therefore, when Ramsbottom read the *The Tiger's Eye* editorial that gave him and the team a no-confidence vote, it was the last straw in an already difficult week. Leaping from his chair, he stormed down the main hallway and out the door to the former army barracks that housed the journalism classroom.

He slammed the door so loud that it startled newspaper advisor Cecile Tanner, a recent college graduate who was starting to build up the quality of *The Tiger's Eye* in the same manner that Ramsbottom had begun to develop the Trimble basketball team twenty-five years ago.

"Miss Tanner, this is an outrage," he blustered, shaking the paper so close to her eyes that she blinked with every syllable. "Which one of your irresponsible students wrote today's editorial? Probably that editor of yours, that prissy-pants Rogers, who keeps the school angry at him half the time. You think things like this are good for our morale? Our team is down and feeling bad enough as it is. How can you let some so-called student expert come out with something so asinine?"

The teacher, although not expecting to hear from Ramsbottom so early in the day, was prepared nonetheless.

"Yes, Coach, the editor steps on a few toes sometimes, but that's what he's supposed to do. And I want you to know that I back him up one hundred percent, especially this time."

"Well, that's just great," Ramsbottom sputtered. "We're the laughing stock of the school already. Why do you have to make matters worse?"

"Our paper doesn't exist to be your PR agent," Miss Tanner replied. "We're here to call things as we see them and to try to make the school better in the process. That's why I allowed the editorial to go through. Because I care about Trimble High, too. I've been to all the games. And I've seen it, just as Clay Rogers says. Your boys are all at odds with each other, and it shows on the court. They don't like each other because they basically don't like themselves. You can tell by the way they treat other people here at school. Sit in Mrs. Hanna's class for just one day and you'll see what I mean. Boys who act like that don't deserve to be champions until they start remembering the kind of stuff that true champions are made of."

Something about the tone of her voice, which hinted of a sincere concern, made Ramsbottom back off a bit and let his anger start to cool. Although still outraged by the editorial and the trouble it would cause him, Ramsbottom also sensed that perhaps Miss Tanner was more of an ally than an enemy.

"Look, Miss Tanner," he muttered, shuffling his size thirteen sneakers on the wooden barracks floor. "I don't like what was written one bit. But I agree with one thing: I do need some help right now. I'm at my wit's end. I don't know what to do to motivate these boys. Nothing I try seems to work."

Finally realizing that without thinking he had bared his soul to this teacher whom he hardly knew, Ramsbottom said, "Okay. Go on. Your staff can write an editorial about that, too. The headline can say, 'Dejected Coach Says He Has No Answers.' But first give me the courtesy of telling me your suggestions before they're put in print. I think I've lost my magic touch—if I ever had one."

"Of course you had one, and you still do," consoled Miss Tanner, much more mellow, now that she could climb off the defensive. "How else would you have won all those championships if you didn't have something special to offer? But sometimes a person can be so close to a problem that he can't really see it. Look, is there maybe someone the boys respect, someone they listen to, whom you could recruit for a little pep talk?"

Ramsbottom thought for a while. He had tried Principal

Gray once before, but that went over badly. The boys associated Gray too closely with punishment, since it was his office that students visited when they were caught in a prank. If enlisted in the cause, Gray would merely come across as another authority figure, which would not be productive just now.

Suddenly, something clicked with Ramsbottom. He had overheard the boys—Freddie, Billy, one of them—mention the new minister in town while they were dressing in the locker room. It was the day that another player, Paul Pemberton, got a new motorcycle for his birthday. The boys asked Paul if he knew that the new minister—what was his name, Meyer or Dyer? Ramsbottom had met him once at the Chamber of Commerce dinner but the name as well as the face had escaped him—had the flashiest Yamaha in town. Said they couldn't believe someone like that, with long hair and a helmet and a cycle, could ever be happy working for a place as dull as a church. When Freddie said he'd almost be willing to go back to church just to hear this guy preach to see if he was for real, Ramsbottom had quaked from surprise.

Ramsbottom himself had not been to church in more than ten years, so he had no idea whether the minister was for real either. When Ramsbottom's children grew up and moved away, he and his wife slipped out of the habit of church attendance. Sunday was usually a big sports day on the tube and Ramsbottom felt he deserved that relaxation.

However, remembering the look of awe on Freddie's face as the boy talked—the idea that any of these self-centered teenagers could have any thought beyond themselves—Ramsbottom was swayed. He suddenly grabbed Miss Tanner's hand and began pumping it in an excited handshake. "You've just given me my answer," Ramsbottom shouted with great relief. "I think I know just the person to call."

Just as quickly as he came in, Ramsbottom backed through the barracks doorway, still flailing his newspaper in the air as he had when she first saw him. Then, as though to make sure he had the last word, the coach reappeared and shouted, "But be careful with the editorials."

Dyer had been on the way out the door to visit hospital patients when Ramsbottom telephoned, and asked him for an appointment.

With little preface to his remarks, Ramsbottom had announced, "I need to find out what makes you so special. I'd just like to know what my players see in you—what makes you hold so much sway over them—since I seem to have run out of steam. They don't go to church, most of them, so it can't be your power in the pulpit. But they talk about you like you're some kind of saint. Just what is it that makes you so persuasive?"

Dyer was intrigued with the proposal and agreed to meet Ramsbottom that afternoon. Somehow, since meeting the boys that day at the soda fountain, Dyer had also sensed that perhaps he could help the team by inspiring the members to look beyond their pettiness and to work together as allies. He had felt a really strong identification with Billy, Freddie, and Beck since that afternoon the four of them had discussed his motorcycle— and he had hoped for an opportunity to get to know them better.

A slight wave of doubt disturbed him, however. Already, in the staid, hidebound congregation of Union Church, he had felt ripples of discontent about his appointment as assistant minister. Besides the board chairman's remarks about his motorcycle that first Sunday, there had been other comments— some subtle and some quite pointed—about his untraditional approach to ministry.

As much as Dyer was flattered by Ramsbottom's interest, the minister wondered how the church members would react if he developed an ongoing relationship with the Tigers. After all, since neither the coach nor many of the players attended Union Church, involving himself with the team could hardly be considered part of the church's ministry.

Yet somehow Dyer felt that in one afternoon's pep talk to a demoralized basketball team, he could accomplish more good than he could delivering a whole month of Sunday sermons. He was willing to go after Ramsbottom's challenge to him, but at what cost he could not say.

5

A Different Kind of Sermon

The plunk-plop-plunk of basketballs bouncing on the gym floor was drowned out by the sputter of John Dyer's motorcycle as he steered his Yamaha into the parking lot outside the Tigers' practice court.

Word of Dyer's impending visit had circulated all day among the team members. By afternoon, curiosity was at a peak, as the boys pondered why the new minister was paying the high-school basketball team a social call.

As the Tigers filed into the locker room and found their seats on the narrow benches, the air was electric with excitement. Something about the event was reminiscent of the first day of school, when students wait with baited breath to size up a new teacher for the first time.

However, along with the excitement came a few predictable murmurs of skepticism. "Why do we have to waste our time listening to a sermon?" Beck had muttered to Paul Pemberton as the two hooked last-minute goals on their way to the locker room. "Seems like another hour on the court this afternoon would help us a lot more."

Ramsbottom tried to appear casual as he greeted Dyer and led him into the locker room, although he knew he would be in the dog house with the players if Dyer's visit turned out to be a bummer. The coach made a nervous attempt at humor while introducing Dyer: "I asked him to come because I thought some divine guidance might help in our current state."

"I don't know about offering divine guidance, Coach," Dyer replied. "I can't promise that, but I can give you some observations as a spectator who has attended all of your games this season. I haven't come to quote Scripture to you, although I'll be happy to give you an earful of Bible verses any time you come to my church. Since I used to play a little basketball myself, I learned something about teamwork that I'd like to pass on."

With that preface, the team members visibly relaxed a bit, since they realized that this would be no session of Bible-thumping. Beck and Paul, who had sneaked in an occasional dribble in the back of the room as Dyer began, ceased their motions, and Dyer seized the hushed moment and plunged in.

"To begin with, I remember from my college days that whenever anything goes wrong, the players automatically blame the coach. They say he's too critical. He's indecisive. He doesn't know what he's doing. He's disorganized. He's calling the wrong plays. He's using the wrong people. I can almost fill in the blanks for you, because I've heard—and even made—some of those same comments during my basketball days, too.

"Well, let me tell you about Coach Ramsbottom here. I've been to every game this season. And to my knowledge, I have not seen him miss a shot, throw a bad pass or let his opponent score a single point."

On the heels of that remark, several players shuffled uncomfortably in their seats. Others merely avoided Dyer's eyes and stared blankly at the floor.

"And I've never been a coach, but I can just imagine the other side of that coin. I can just suspect what might go on in a coach's mind about now, too. The coach might think, 'The players don't care. They don't concentrate. They're in it for themselves. They're simply on ego trips.' And the list of complaints goes on.

"Well, in a way, coaches who say things like that may be right, since the team members aren't perfect either. And goodness knows that sitting at the helm of a bunch of boisterous teenagers isn't the world's most pleasant occupation. But how many years has it been since a coach today was a teenager! Can a coach today really know what kinds of pressure that modern young people are up against?"

Ramsbottom nodded his head slowly, as Dyer's words struck a disquietingly familiar chord. He could see that Dyer's talk would be pointed at him, too. But instead of reacting defensively, Ramsbottom promised himself to try to stay open-minded and hear Dyer out.

"So, with this in mind, I want to tell you about a two-part program that may help you as you strive to turn your losing situation around. The first part includes things for you each to do as individuals. The second phase is for you to try as a team."

Dyer took a piece of chalk and began making marks on the chalkboard, although his marks were strikingly different from the coach's game diagrams the boys were accustomed to seeing.

Under Roman numeral I, he wrote the words *Team Goal* and then the words *Personal Goal.* He noted that the team had eleven games left for the regular season and could go on to the play-offs only if they finished the season in the top four.

The Tigers were at that point 0–5. To finish in the top four, the Tigers would have to end up 9–7 for the season, or at the absolute worst, 8–8. That meant that the Tigers would have to win at least eight, and preferably nine, of their last eleven games.

"I want you to go home tonight and write down what you want your team goal to be for the rest of the year," he said. "What you must do is decide whether you like being last or whether you want to see what it's like up closer to the top. Remember that two of those eleven games that are left are with Randolph, and they haven't lost a game this year. So if two of your allowable losses are to Randolph, that leaves you only one more loss at the absolute most—if you even want to think about the play-offs. What do you hope to achieve teamwise? Think about it and write it down."

Under the category of personal goals, Dyer suggested that the team members steer away from answering this in terms of points they hope to score.

"If you concentrate on things like rebounding better and defending and hustling harder, you will find that your point total will come around on its own. Under personal goals, be as specific as you can. Don't say that you are merely going to 'do better' or 'try harder.' Think of specific things that you can do to improve your individual game."

Under Roman numeral II, Dyer wrote the words *Motion Picture.*

"Now this may look like I'm suggesting you spend three evenings a week down at the Bijou seeing the latest movie instead of practicing your game," Dyer joked. "But the motion picture I want you to see doesn't cost you a penny, because it's going to be on the movie screen of your mind."

He urged the boys to visualize themselves accomplishing the actual goals, both team and personal, that they had written on paper.

"Picture the Tigers playing and winning games against your opponents. See the scoreboard and the happy faces of the fans and your teammates. Picture your team against your archrival, Randolph, playing well and winning. Picture the team as you

carry Coach Ramsbottom off the court after a victorious game.
Picture the fans driving out of the parking lot, tooting their
horns and waving their streamers in a victory celebration.

"Visualize yourself shooting well from the field and foul
line. See yourself aggressively playing defense and rebounding,
scrambling after loose balls, cutting to openings, hustling the
whole game. Play over those pictures in your mind and try
to catch the excitement and satisfaction you feel when you've
done your best."

Next, he wrote *Bedside* under Roman numeral III. "And
this doesn't mean that I want you to sleep on the job," he
teased.

Instead, he urged the boys to review the first two parts of
the plan each night before bedtime and then analyze what
each player feels is keeping him from accomplishing those
goals.

"For instance, maybe you have trouble playing well in the
last quarter of your games. You come on with great exuberance,
but then you fade in the final minutes. So focus on this for
a few minutes. See a scoreboard showing your team ahead
in the last quarter and see yourself playing at full strength.
To make this a reality, decide that you are going to try to
work your hardest the last fifteen minutes of practice each
day. See yourself becoming stronger. At the same time, work
to build up your endurance for those final minutes. In short,
what you must do is to combine positive thinking with positive
doing.

"What I'm telling you will work for you, not only in basketball, but in everything you do in life. Many people never set
definite goals. They formulate some hazy kind of outline, such
as 'I promise to work harder this year,' but they never stay
with it for any longer than a few days. Be specific and actually
see yourself accomplishing that plan.

"Maybe that can mean the championship; maybe it will
just mean third place; or maybe you won't even make the

play-offs. But the main thing is to move toward the best that is in you and then you will see some rewards. The reason that you don't feel good about basketball and each other right now is that you know you are not doing the best that you can."

With those points made, Dyer paused to make a mental sweep of the room and note how his words were being received. The boys were quiet and attentive, and even the usual nay-sayers had stopped their fidgeting. A couple of players had begun taking notes, and Dyer felt comfortable in pushing on with the lecture.

"The next part of the plan is a little harder, because it will require a thorough readjustment of the way you view life right now," he began. "There are some rules involved here, and for some of you, they will be especially strict ones." Dyer told the team that every member, from the coach to the water boy, must begin building team organization on the basis of encouragement and "brotherly love."

"Brotherly love," Dyer repeated for the boys, pausing to mull over those words for a moment. "Now that's an archaic phrase for you. Hasn't been heard since William Penn's day, has it? But it's a good term. Just dust it off a little. It applies to the Trimble Tigers in the same way Penn applied it to the city of Philadelphia."

"Under this plan, only the coach will be allowed to criticize players' mistakes and he will try to do so only in the most positive way possible," Dyer instructed.

"He will try not to continue the criticism any further than is necessary and will shift toward showing what *should* be done, as soon as a mistake is pointed out," he said. "You players must not resent the coach's criticism, because it is necessary if you are to learn. And the criticism will only be given privately, not out loud with half the town listening."

Predictably, Ramsbottom reddened at this remark, but just as quickly, he gave the boys a sheepish smile. Dyer knew it was a gamble to make this oblique reference to Ramsbottom's mid-game theatrics, but he viewed it as a necessary risk in getting his point across.

Promptly, he then turned back to the players.

"Each player from the top man to the last substitute will try to give encouragement to his teammates. He will tell his neighbor when he thinks he did a good job on defense or when he made a good pass. No negative remarks will be allowed among the players, either privately or face to face. If some deep problem occurs, go to Coach Ramsbottom and ask him to help the two or three of you involved to work it out. On a routine basis, if you can't say something nice, don't say it at all. You don't have to be insincere, and you don't have to give credit where credit is not due. But surely, you can always find someone to praise for something he is doing well—if you look around hard enough."

Dyer urged the boys to try to greet each new practice time enthusiastically and give their best during that ninety minutes every day.

"Take today. Maybe your favorite yellow Izod shirt acquired a grape-juice stain at breakfast. Maybe your girl friend walked to class with your best friend. Maybe you bombed out on your math test this afternoon. Those things are bad news, and they can really defeat you if you let them. You may feel like slacking off in practice today, just because you're mad at life. But promise yourself that you won't. You can sulk later. You can clean the juice stain later. You can call your best girl tonight and iron out the problem. But these ninety minutes of practice won't happen again for another day. Dedicate yourself to your best effort."

Dyer told the boys that his last requirement would take more work than any of the previous ones, and would be even more difficult than winning the championship itself.

"I am asking you to begin thinking of each other as brothers. When any good thing happens to one of you, it happens to all of you. If Clark here gets the gold star for being the high scorer of the evening, it's a compliment to the entire team.

"In playing basketball, as in most things in life, your own success is increased by the success of those around you. You are all working for the same general goals. And what you are together is more than what you are individually. You have great power as a group. You must believe in that power. It will be magnified when you work together. Encourage each other in an enthusiastic program with a regard—no, the word I want to use is stronger than that—with a *love* in your hearts for each other.

"Now some of you may be saying, 'There is no way I could love Billy Williams or Freddie Malone or Coach Ramsbottom or Joe Campus or whomever. Well, first try to love yourself and want the very best for yourself. Then realize that the player next to you is a person, too."

Dyer began passing out some 3″ x 5″ cards on which he had printed the program he had just outlined.

"I've given you my program and my pep talk. But I'm leaving you in good hands. Coach Ramsbottom will check up on you—and I might say that you will check up on him—to see how well everyone is doing. I expect great things from you. I want you to expect great things from yourselves, too."

With that, Dyer shook the coach's hand, then walked toward the door. At first, there was only a smattering of applause. But as Dyer glanced briefly over his shoulder to wave good-bye, he saw a few players starting to stand while they clapped. Then a few others rose. In seconds, the whole team was on its feet, applauding enthusiastically.

Dyer did not stick around to bask in the glory of the standing ovation and the admiration of the players for the speech he had just made. With one last wave, he was out the door and revving up his Yamaha for the ride back to the church. What was said, was said. It was now up to Ramsbottom and the team to pick up the gauntlet if they wished to follow through on his challenging suggestions.

Ramsbottom, relieved that his eleventh-hour decision to invite Dyer had been a success, stayed on his feet as the players replanted themselves on the benches. For once, on the heels of Dyer's comments, it was hard to look the players in the eye.

"You may find it hard to believe," Ramsbottom finally said. "But some of the things Reverend Dyer asked us to do will be harder for me than for anyone here. But I promise you that if you will try, I will, too. I don't have much else to say. The reverend has said it all for me. But we do have a few minutes of practice time left in the day. Let's not waste the rest of the afternoon. So go out on the court, form two lines, and do some warm-up exercises."

The sun from the unseasonably warm December day beamed down on Dyer's motorcycle helmet as he motored out of the high-school parking lot. Something about the past few minutes had made the minister feel all warm inside, too. His speech to the Trimble Tigers had been as satisfying as any sermon he had preached in his entire career. It was thrilling for him to be able to combine his past ardor for basketball with his present skills in the ministry. He found himself humming over the roar of his motorcycle and feeling genuinely happy for the first time since—well, since Lucy died.

Suddenly Dyer became aware of a white car inching its way along behind him—the same white car that had been in his rear-view mirror since he left Trimble High. Along Grant Avenue, as he rode the mile or so to the Altamont intersection, the white car stayed on his bumper, trailing him as he pulled into the Union Church parking lot.

Dyer hopped off the Yamaha and turned around to identify the driver. Peering closely, he saw it was Charley Graves, chairman of the board of deacons at the church.

"Why, Charley—was that you following me?" Dyer finally asked, a little relieved to see he was in no danger. "I thought for a moment it was a mugger on my tail."

"You bet it was me," Graves proclaimed somewhat testily

as he bounded out of the white car and walked over to face Dyer. "Couldn't believe my eyes when I saw you ridin' that motorcycle out of the high-school parking lot on a Friday afternoon. Isn't this your day to make hospital calls? Poor Mrs. Blackstone called me this morning just cryin' to high heaven. Said it had been two whole days since you've been by to see her. I was comin' by the church to see if you were sick or something. Then I see you zoomin' along like some hippie, ridin' away from Trimble High. That's an unlikely place for a preacher to be. What are you doin'? Going over there teachin' those youngsters how to be thugs?"

Dyer gaped at Graves incredulously. "I sure hope you're kidding, Charley, but something about your voice says you're not. I was at Trimble this afternoon because Coach Ramsbottom asked me to talk to the basketball players. He thought maybe an encouraging word from someone outside the school would do them good. And as for Mrs. Blackstone, I was planning to stop by the hospital on my way home."

Graves was not appeased. "It's not a minister's place to be hobnobbin' with the basketball team. Let the coach give his own pep talk if he wants his kids inspired. Those boys haven't darkened the door of Union Church in months, and when they do, they're such troublemakers everyone hopes they never come back. You're wastin' your time, not to mention the church's, when you go over there, you know. We didn't hire you to be a cheerleader."

Something about the "We didn't hire you" had a hollow ring to it. Although Graves did not say it, he might as well have added, "And we also can fire you." But Graves did not stick around to add anything. His speech finished, he hopped behind the wheel of the white car and sped away.

On his way to visit the team, Dyer had wondered what price he would pay for getting involved with the Tigers. Now he wondered if Graves had just hinted at the answer.

6

The Winds of Change

The impact of John Dyer's words remained convincingly strong as the next few weeks went by at Trimble High School.

For the team members, Dyer's speech breathed new life into sagging spirits. The motivational goals that Dyer outlined for the boys gave them something on which to concentrate besides their complaints and their nitpicking with each other.

For example, Freddie Malone had listed as his personal goal to practice his free throws for an extra fifteen minutes each day. In just one week's time, Freddie was hitting most of his shots right on the money, instead of failing at more than half as he had done the first few weeks of the season.

Clark Symons's goal was even more amazing to his teammates. He wrote down that he would try to pass more often and stop hogging the ball when others were in a better position to score. To his surprise, while following this credo, Symons ended up with the ball more than ever during practice time, since players like Billy and Beck began reciprocating when they saw that Symons was now willing to share the limelight.

Perhaps the biggest change of all was seen in Coach Rams-bottom, who had written on his goal card that he would give each of the boys one hour of his personal time in the next two weeks. "I guess I had lost track of the fact that these boys are people with real needs and real problems, not just basketball machines," the coach confided to Dyer a few days after the minister's visit, when Ramsbottom telephoned Dyer to thank him for the speech.

"Some of the boys told me about how they struggle just to get their parents to say one kind word to them during a day. Some of them talked about how hard it is to learn calculus. Others even opened up to me about their love life. Can you believe it? After just one or two conferences, I began to realize that although I spend about ninety minutes every day with these boys, I never really knew them.

"Get a load of this one. Beck Beckwith told me that the one thing he wants in all the world is a motorcycle. With all the money his dad has, old man Beckwith won't buy him a cycle. Doesn't think they're safe. The guy just gets green with envy every time he sees you drive by."

On this note, practices began changing dramatically, as players remembered their promise to find things to praise about each other and to lay low on the negatives. For the first few sessions, telling one's teammate that he made a good shot or defended his opponent well was excruciating for some of the players, who never before had anything but barbs for the other team members as they went to the showers.

At first, the locker room was strangely quiet after practice, with players being extremely guarded for fear they would be teased unmercifully for any conversation that was not typical locker-room banter. But gradually, old habits fell, and Billy was even overheard to tell Clark, his archrival, "Hey buddy you really looked sharp on that lay-up."

The Tigers won their next four games, which came as a surprise to no one who had watched their much-inspired practices and had witnessed their improved attitude. The town newspaper's sports columnist called the Tigers "a team newly born" and said their recent successes were "a turnaround cure."

Moreover, as the Tigers' lot improved, the whole attitude of the school seemed to be revived by the winds of change which blew through the halls. Even Mrs. Hanna, who had so often been harassed by the players during the height of the team's frustration, was feeling the benefits of the team's upswing. It had been several weeks now since the boys had pulled the wastebasket-on-the-window-ledge routine, and she had actually been able to cover an entire unit in Spanish without asking anyone to conjugate extra verbs as punishment.

There was yet another and stranger development which was a direct spin-off of Dyer's visit. Beck, Billy, and Freddie became curious about what Dyer was like when he wore clerical garb, so they decided to try returning to church for the first time since their barnyard sounds hastened Reverend Meth's departure the previous summer.

On their first Sunday back, the boys were surprised to see the usually empty classroom quite crowded, as other curiosity-seekers filed in to hear the new young preacher whose reputation was fast spreading throughout town.

Dyer was already into his lesson on the Lord's Prayer and was talking about people's tendency to concentrate on their past mistakes.

"Once you have realized an error for what it is and want to try to change it, you need not worry about your failure any longer," he said. "As a human, you must recognize your blunders as being a part of life. Failing to accept forgiveness for errors and losses will keep you from living in a happy manner today. You will then tend to repeat the same mistakes over and over because these errors remain on your mind.

"For example, if I told you right now not to think about elephants for the next five minutes, you would be sure to think of elephants. You see, you have already done so. Why? Because putting a negative word in front of the thought will not change the basic thought. You still see elephants.

"If you want to change your thinking, you must plug in a brand-new thought. That is, if you don't want to think about elephants, tell yourself that you are only going to think of ships in the ocean for the next few minutes.

"The point is, if you are concentrating on your past mistakes, you can live only in those thoughts, and they affect your behavior because your mind is capable of acting on only one thought at a time. Doing this is self-defeating because you prevent yourself from giving proper attention to today's needs.

"If you accept forgiveness for yourself, then you can also forgive others because you feel your own forgiveness. When we feel badly toward ourselves, we invariably take it out on others. Watch a little boy who gets scolded by his parents. Most often he will try to take out his resentment on the next child or object he encounters. He does not yet know about forgiveness. A self-forgiving person with a healthy self-image is free to forgive others and to love others, because he has found it easier to accept himself.

"Jesus asks that one not be led toward temptations of evil and destructive things, but that each person be directed to positive things. Here He reveals again the power of the mind to control our actions. The power of positive thinking is well over 2,000 years old. Jesus is saying that each person must try to keep his or her mind off negative, destructive ideas.

"In other words, Jesus says that we ought to ask for and 'think on' the things that are creative and winning, an attitude which can lead us toward the highest of our goals in terms of happy lives and relationships."

As the class ended and the boys walked away, Beck murmured, "Sure beats the daylights out of the old hellfire-and-damnation routine that I remember."

Even though Trimble had beaten its last four opponents and things were looking up—with a season record of 4–5 now—

they had still not played Randolph, their old archenemy. And somehow the Tigers, as well as the school and the town, considered this the crucial test of whether Trimble was really an improved team, or whether the past four games had been just a fluke.

The three days before the Randolph game were somewhat akin to the days before the Christmas holidays. Concentrating on classwork was impossible as excitement built to a fever pitch. Spirit banners and posters were abundant, and it became a challenge just to walk through the hallways without bumping into paper chains that seemed to be draped from one end of the building to another.

For several nights, basketball practice after school extended well into the evening, and Ramsbottom drilled the boys so hard that they went home exhausted.

As the coach walked through the front door of Trimble High on the morning of the Randolph game, several small groups of students gathered in the entry way cheered enthusiastically, and others slapped him on the back and shouted, "Yea, Coach. You're our hero."

Ramsbottom smiled, obviously tickled that his stock had risen so sharply in the past few weeks and marveling at the contrast from the day he arrived at school to find himself maligned in *The Tiger's Eye.* In fact, he was sure that was why Miss Tanner, the journalism teacher, had left a note in his mailbox asking him to stop by her office when he arrived at school that morning. Ramsbottom had concluded that the newspaper advisor was now regretting the harsh words of the editorial several weeks ago and was offering to apologize in light of the team's recent victories.

"Okay, Miss Tanner," Ramsbottom began as he sauntered into the journalism classroom. "What does it take to get a good editorial out of *The Tiger's Eye?* After we beat Randolph tonight, I bet you'll be forced to admit that the Tigers are a pretty good bunch of guys after all." However, one look at

Miss Tanner's face told Ramsbottom that a retraction was the last thing on the advisor's mind.

"I wish I could do that. I really do," Miss Tanner sighed hesitatingly. "But I'm afraid I have some facts that indicate that just the opposite is true."

"Now what does a statement like that mean?" Ramsbottom demanded, wedging his hefty frame down into a student desk.

"I've had our investigative team following a lead for several weeks now. They came back yesterday with some pretty firm facts, and the way their story shapes up, things aren't looking so good for the Tigers after all."

Ramsbottom found himself growing angry fast. "What lead?" he barked. "And what do these so-called facts have to do with my team?"

Miss Tanner lowered herself into a student desk, too, so she could maintain eye contact with the belligerent coach.

"It all started when one of our reporters got word that the sheriff's office planned to send their drug-sniffing dog to Trimble High. The reporter went up to Center City to write a feature on the dog, thinking it was simply a human-interest item; you know, a real laugh-a-minute story that the sheriff was checking for drugs here on this small-town campus. At first it just looked as if the sheriff was conducting a routine, precautionary check.

"Well, the reporter kept asking questions about the dog and badgering the sheriff. We've been studying about how reporters need to look beyond the 'party line' that bureaucrats are forever spouting. So, when he kept asking questions, he found out that, well, it wasn't just a lark after all. The sheriff has tips that there really is a drug scene at Trimble High. And the dog is coming here tomorrow to begin checking things out."

Ramsbottom was at once on his feet. "Oh, I see it all now," he said sarcastically. "You've decided that the whole basketball team is somehow in on this. My players, whom I don't think you've ever really liked, are the guilty parties. Am I right?"

"No, not all your players, Coach," Miss Tanner replied. "But, I'm sorry to say, I believe a few of them are."

"And what exactly do you base that accusation on?" Ramsbottom shot back. "You'd better be careful, ma'am. I may coach basketball, but I know a little something about newspapers, and you can libel people with those kinds of remarks."

"And libel is defensible by truth," Miss Tanner said. "My reporter didn't stop with the sheriff's office. He stumbled on a source who had some contacts with the underground. He was told that one of the key links to the drug supply line on the Trimble campus is one of the players on the Trimble basketball team."

"You're out of your mind, lady," Ramsbottom shouted. "There aren't any basketball players doing drugs. I'm sure of it. I'd know it if they were. I'm with them all the time. I. . . ."

"I didn't say someone was *doing* drugs. I just said that one of your players was apparently implicated as a link to getting the drugs to the students. There's no indication that he's an actual user. But being a conduit is trouble enough."

"All right, all right," Ramsbottom said. "Just suppose, which I don't, that your accusation is true. Come forth with the facts. Name names. Give times, dates. Be specific. You're in the newspaper business. I want to hear the facts. If you're going to make a charge, spell it out."

"I can't. And neither can my reporter. His source wasn't about to go that far, just in case he was talking to a snitch. But we do have two clues. In the first place, it has to be someone whose circle of contacts is wider than just Trimble— somebody who hangs out with people who are from another city, maybe even another country. In a place the size of Trimble, you can be pretty sure that things don't just originate here. And second, it has to be someone poor; someone who doesn't have any money to call his own. Apparently the sole motive for being the conduit is funds, since it's very unlikely that the person is a drug user himself."

Ramsbottom thought a minute. "Poor student? I don't have anyone who is poor, or at least nobody who lets on. Come to think of it, I don't think we ever discussed anyone's economic status. But certainly there's nobody who's destitute enough to turn to drugs for cash. Why, if someone has been hurting for funds, they could have automatically asked me. I can't give them much. I mean, I'm just the basketball coach, not an oil company exec. But I surely could tide someone over until payday, or until his parents' next dole."

Miss Tanner could see that she was making no headway and that arguing with Ramsbottom was senseless. If he wanted to bury his head in the sand and ignore the problem, she was not responsible for protecting him. But she thought one final warning was in order.

"Look, Coach. I'm ready to go to the principal's office with this story. And we'll go into print with it, depending on what he says. I wish I could nip it in the bud by prompting the school to take some action, so that the story never has to run in *The Tiger's Eye*. But if the principal takes the same ostrich approach as you seem to be, I'll have no choice.

"Our facts are good. Our sources are good. We feel confident that we have the right set of data. Our function is to keep the public informed, and maybe a story like this will keep people here from being susceptible to drugs, once they realize that the officials are serious about tracking down the abusers.

"But I thought I owed you the courtesy of telling you first before it's in the paper. I'm really sorry. I wish there were something I could do."

Ramsbottom said nothing. Miss Tanner obviously had the upper hand in this conversation, and there was no talking her out of pursuing the matter, even though her data obviously contained many holes. His only hope was for a stall.

"Look, Miss Tanner," the coach offered. "You're determined to go ahead with your story. I can't stop that. But please just give me the courtesy of letting me talk to the team first.

Tonight's the big game with Randolph. If I approached them now, it would ruin everything. We have to beat Randolph. It means everything, don't you see? We've come so far in the past few weeks. Morale is at an all-time high. This would destroy all that. I promise. I'll talk to the team after the game. Just let me handle this my way."

Miss Tanner agreed to keep her information under wraps and hold off visiting the principal until the next day.

"Coach, don't get me wrong. I don't like this any better than you do. I tried to dismiss the very idea at first and write it all off as this reporter's overzealousness. But the student started bringing in facts that I couldn't ignore. And you can't either, if you really care for your team and this school. We can't sit here and know that drugs are infiltrating our school and do nothing about it."

Ramsbottom made a quick exit and slipped back to the gym before anyone could see his chalk-white face. He had to regain his composure before any of the boys came in. He just hoped he could keep his cool until after tonight's game, because he needed to buy some time to figure out the best way to broach the subject to the team.

Somebody who had contacts outside of Trimble, Miss Tanner had said. Somebody who needed money of his own. Ramsbottom called the roll of the team members in his mind, unable to believe that any of his Tigers could possibly fit into this sordid description.

Suddenly a very sick feeling came over Ramsbottom as he started down the team roster a second time. The coach first shook his head frantically, as though he could shake bad thoughts from his mind by swift physical motion.

Then he picked up the telephone and dialed what was becoming a familiar number. Once again, Ramsbottom had a problem that needed John Dyer's attention.

7

A Loser of a Deal

By some miracle, the Tigers and Randolph were tied 58–58 at the end of the third quarter.

Ramsbottom had watched his team, which had been so fired up and so on target during the past four games, slip very gradually back into the slump that had plagued them when they suffered that disastrous loss to North Side several weeks ago. The teamwork that had spurred the players to four consecutive victories after John Dyer's talk had seemed to erode this evening in front of Ramsbottom's very eyes.

By the half, Clark and Billy were snarling at each other in the dressing room and seemed to be back to their old competitive antics.

"Well, we are right back where we started," whined Billy, as he entered the dressing room at half-time when the Tigers trailed 38–35. "We don't rebound, we don't pass, and we can't make it in the clutch."

"Yeah, you should talk, big mouth," Clark barked back at him. "What did you do besides miss a hundred shots during the second quarter?"

But Billy and Clark were not the only ones who were out of sync on this crucial evening. Freddie had been dull on his free throws for the first time in recent weeks. And the whole team, which had been buoyed by overconfidence and had persuaded Ramsbottom to cut practices short a few days during the past week, now looked sluggish as a result.

Ramsbottom felt lifeless and out of sorts, too. As the game began, he had tried to shrug off the events of the morning. But try as he might, Ramsbottom knew that the worry and anguish that had mounted all day were preventing him from coaching effectively. Instead of his usual bench-side theatrics and sarcasm, however, Ramsbottom spent most of the game slumped in his chair, with his mind wandering.

On the advice of John Dyer, the coach had deliberately kept Miss Tanner's news about the drug investigation under his hat for now. Dyer had persuaded the coach not to storm right in and air the dirty linen to the team at practice that afternoon, but to be judicious and wait until a more opportune time.

"The boys are up for the game and they need this win," cautioned Dyer. "You'll destroy them if you blow up now. At least wait until after they play Randolph tonight before you start interrogating them."

Ramsbottom had tried to shoulder all the blame for any drug involvement that the players might have. "I just found out how to get close to these boys. We were just starting to talk. I was just beginning to find out what their lives were like," he moaned. "And now it may be too late. If some of our players have been messing around with drugs, it's my fault for not picking up on some warning signs."

"I wouldn't be too hard on myself if I were you, Coach," Dyer replied. "It's impossible to gauge all the good and the bad that we do as we go through life. The main thing is to try to do the best that we can today. Even with the noblest of intentions, we all know so little about life that we can never be sure of everything. A person must not pressure himself too much. Just make an effort to realize the best that is in you and try to give out some love every chance you get. Remember that whatever happens now with the team, you can handle it. Your players need you now more than ever. And I'll do whatever I can to support you if there's a crisis."

The last quarter was largely a blur to Ramsbottom, since he somehow had an ominous feeling about how the game would end. He also knew the job that awaited him when the buzzer sounded.

To no one's surprise, the Tigers soon blew their 58–56 third-quarter lead. A heavy Randolph press forced the Tigers into many errors which allowed the Pirates to dominate the last few minutes by scoring the final ten points in the game. The last stanza ended with the score of Randolph 82, Trimble 68, but Ramsbottom was by now so mortified at the thought of talking to his team about the drug story that he did not even hear the boos of the hometown crowd as the bad news flashed on the scoreboard.

John Dyer was standing outside the locker room when the downcast Ramsbottom left the gym floor and turned the corner to enter. Dyer put his hands firmly on the coach's shoulders as though the simple gesture would be enough to restrain him.

"Just wait a few minutes more, Coach," Dyer cautioned. "Let me talk to them first."

"But I want to. . . ." Ramsbottom stammered, somehow reluctant to let Dyer break the news.

"Okay, I'll let you. You can be the one, I promise. But I want to talk to them about the game. Please. I think it will help."

They entered the locker room just in time to see Billy slowly move toward Clark, his hands curled into sullen fists hanging by his side. "I'll tell you a thing or two. . . ." Billy started.

Dyer's raised voice drowned Billy out. "I'll tell you a thing or two," he mimicked with a slight smile that stopped Billy in his tracks and diverted the players from watching the fight that they thought was imminent. "You guys are still all right. It was a tough game to lose after winning four in a row. But let's look to see where we are now. You have won 80 percent of your last five games. A few weeks ago you had to go nine–two or eight–three to get in the play-offs and you still had two games with Randolph. Now you have only one game left with them, and you need to go only five–one or four–two. No matter how bleak things may seem tonight, you are still making progress."

The hostile little groups that had begun to form in the locker room, as in former days, started to dissipate as Dyer spoke, commanding the same attention that he did the first time he visited Trimble. Sensing that he was being heard despite the near ruckus, the minister continued:

"Tonight, you have had a temporary setback. Maybe you slacked off on your thinking or on working harder in practice. Maybe you got a little careless with success. Maybe you got a little overconfident.

"I'm just curious about something. How many of you missed a few times this past week in reading your goal cards and in taking some time to form the pictures in your minds that we talked about? Please, please. No show of hands. You know who you are. But each of you take time and answer this question to yourselves, because it's an important one.

"Look, nothing worthwhile comes easily. The laws of nature favor the person who stays with a task through difficulty as well as through success. You have learned two great lessons in a short time. One is that you can change your situation by changing your thoughts. The other is that it is as important to continue working through your successes as it is to work to get out of your pattern of failing in the first place.

"You can't let temporary losses defeat you, and you can't allow limited success cause you to become lazy. Although it's necessary to be able to relax and enjoy success, a person must also check from time to time to be sure he is still moving toward the best that is in him. Make the most of your life by mixing your fun moments and your work, and don't forget to do them both. When you relax, let go. When you work, work hard. You are improving, and you need only to get back to the basics a little each day and things will turn out well."

With the players still hushed from his speech, Dyer went around the benches briefly and spoke a sentence or two to each person. An amazing calm settled over the room, compared to the electrified atmosphere that the coach had encountered when he first walked in.

When Dyer had finished his rounds, he turned to Ramsbottom and said, "Coach, they're all yours. I didn't mean to take so much time. I turn the meeting over to you."

With his heart suddenly beating so loudly he was sure it could be heard in the next room, Ramsbottom slowly surveyed the group. Now it was his turn to lay on the heavy talk, to tell the boys that tonight's loss to Randolph was merely the beginning of their troubles, to grill each player individually about his potential role in a drug scene.

However, observing the mollified, almost peaceful looks on the boys' faces, he backed down.

"No, Reverend, you've said it all better than I could even begin to try. The boys don't need a lecture tonight. You've given us plenty to think about. Let's all go home and get a good night's sleep and get ready for a good practice tomorrow afternoon."

Visibly relieved, although unaware of the real lecture that they missed, the players began drifting out to the showers.

Dyer shot Ramsbottom a quizzical look as the two men walked to the door. "I just can't do this to them," he replied before the question was even asked. "I'll handle it another way, on a one-to-one basis."

"I think that's a wise decision," Dyer affirmed. "But how are you going to know where to start?"

"John, I may have gotten into this game of getting to know my players in the last quarter, so to speak. But I've come in ready to make up for lost time. And if the puzzle piece doesn't fit, we all know it won't be my first royal boo-boo."

Both men managed a weak laugh at that remark. Dyer shook the coach's hand, wished him good luck and left.

The boys slowly finished showering and drifted out in their usual groups. Ramsbottom sat in his office until the last players were departing.

Beck seemed to be dragging his heels abnormally long tonight. When he finally finished his clean-up, Ramsbottom said to him, "Oh, Beckwith, could you stop by here a minute? I'm going to need your help."

Instantly defensive, Beck shot back, "I know, Coach. You don't have to remind me. I was lousy on my passes tonight. And I'm sure you think I gave Billy the ball too much. But John's right. I got overconfident this week and let down my guard. I'll do better, I promise."

"Okay, Beckwith, okay. I accept your promise. But that's not the favor I need the most."

"Huh?" the player asked. "I don't get it."

So Ramsbottom very methodically told Beckwith about his conversation with Miss Tanner, about how her reporter was tipped off to an upcoming drug shipment into Trimble, about how some unidentifed member of the basketball team had been recruited as a conduit to get the drugs onto campus, and that Miss Tanner was sitting on this news at that very moment, ready to take it up with the principal just as soon as Ramsbottom had discussed the matter with the team.

Beck's face went instantly white. "Drugs on our team?" he stammered. "That's ridiculous. That newspaper has always hated us. They've written ugly things about us all year. Just exactly what proof do they have to back up their accusations?"

"Apparently pretty sound proof," Ramsbottom replied. "One of their reporters actually went undercover for several

weeks, and Miss Tanner feels that they have a good picture
of the local effort. Miss Tanner would have gone to the principal today, except that I begged her to hold up so I could
talk to the team."

"Talk to the team?" Beck gasped. "You're not going to
do that, are you? I mean, after how badly things went tonight
and all? Do you really think there's a reason for everyone to
know?"

"I did at first, but now I'm not so sure," said Ramsbottom.
"But here's where I need your help. Beck, you've got a lot
of friends on the team. You're an insider. Furthermore, you're
a curious sort, and sometimes I think you've got bloodhound
instincts—even on the court where you can snoop around and
find the right openings."

"I didn't do so well at that tonight," Beck said, again defensive.

"No, but nobody did, including the coach," Ramsbottom
replied. "But we will again, just as John Dyer said. And you'll
get back to bird-dogging those balls. I just know you will.
In the meantime, we've got a more pressing problem. I need
you to help me find out what this is all about. If we've got
troubles, I want to face up to it. But let's do it now, while
the ball is still in our court and not in the principal's office.
Or worse yet, in the sheriff's department."

Beck nodded his assent, grabbed his dirty clothes, and
quickly darted for the door.

Here Ramsbottom cornered him again.

"Oh, Beck, just one more thing. I'd like to end this conversation on a more cheerful subject. Gene Symons down at the
sporting-goods store contacted me today. He's looking for some
stockroom help on weekends and two days after school, and
he can't hire Clark because Clark needs the time to work on
his grades.

"I guess it may seem funny, but I thought you might like
to try for the job. I know you're not exactly the neediest person

on the team. But I remembered our conversation about the motorcycle. I know your dad has said he won't fund a bike for you. How about it? Would you like to take a stab at that job? Or should I ask someone else?"

Beck was momentarily stunned. He'd never had a part-time job before—or any job, for that matter—and the idea of the coach's recommendation of the town's richest kid almost had a streak of humor in it. But Beck was not laughing.

"Gosh, Coach, are you sure he'll hire me? I mean, I don't have much work experience."

"If you want the job, you'll come with my heartiest recommendation. I've found you to be quite trainable," said Ramsbottom.

Beck alternately sighed, smiled his thanks, and then looked at his watch nervously. Without further conversation, he bounded out the door, running the full length of the gym despite his exhaustion from the game.

Maybe it was his imagination. But Ramsbottom was sure he detected a sigh of relief in the boy's parting gesture.

The navy van—with the Hawaiian girl dancing the hula painted on one side—had been sitting on the Trimble parking lot just east of the gym for more than an hour now. Partially blocked by the bricked-off garbage area, the van was pulled far enough forward so that the dejected Trimble fans could be seen coming from the gym as the game ended.

Although the players should be emerging from their locker rooms approximately half an hour later, the time passed and nothing happened. Something seemed to be dragging the action tonight. For what seemed like an eternity, no one came out at all. Then a thin, long-haired man exited from the dressing area and sped off on a gigantic black Yamaha.

Some time after that, freshly showered players began drifting out, some meeting girl friends who had been gathered just inside the hallway of the gym.

Still moments ticked away, and more waiting, waiting. He

had never been late before, but that was just talk. Tonight, when it really mattered—the make-or-break meeting, when the stakes were really high—he was running late. Did he not know that every minute counted in this business, especially now since the high school had recently hired a security guard to patrol the school area?

More minutes passed. A portly older man, still dressed in his sweaty game shirt, finally came out of the locker room, turned out all the lights, and locked the door behind him.

Now what could that mean? Had the kid forgotten them, on the very night when they had brought him his long-awaited dole? They would stay in the parking lot for fifteen more minutes, and that was the limit. Just in case he was hiding out somewhere to make doubly sure the coast was clear.

The gym lights flickered off and the janitor locked up the building and drove off in his old pickup. The parking lot was empty now. And there had been no action.

The navy van with the Hawaiian girl painted on the side slowly ground through the parking lot, with its lights still off.

8

Success and Storm Clouds

John Dyer looked out the window of his study and took in the beauty of the elm tree whose branches were bent down with snow on this wintry February day. The icy scene was a tangible reminder to Dyer of how many months had gone by since the day of his first meeting with Beck, Billy, and Freddie at the drugstore as the trio downed Alice Smoot's sodas to cool off from the hot summer weather.

Looking back on that meeting, Dyer realized how much his relationship with the basketball team had expanded in the intervening months. In his new role as the Tigers' unofficial chaplain and chief morale booster, Dyer had found more enthusiasm for life than he had in anything since Lucy died.

No longer did he dread getting out of bed every morning and facing a new day alone. Every new sunrise reached out as a new challenge, and his own energies were renewed and replenished.

Furthermore, Dyer was happier now in his work at the church than at any other job he had ever held. For the first time in his life, Dyer truly believed that he was in the right place, doing the exact work that God intended for him to do.

Largely because of his reputation with the basketball team, young people who had never been to church, plus many who had been absent for years, began filling the pews on Sundays. Dyer felt his sermons grow sharper and more eloquent because he now knew he was addressing a specific need.

Dyer knew he was still not tops on everyone's list. There were still some grumblings, mainly from people who were jealous of his popularity and did not cotton to his long hair and motorcycle. There were still a handful of church members who felt that Dyer's pep talks to the team were improper and who thought he should stay away from the school.

But, by and large, the town of Trimble credited him with the turnaround that the team was beginning to make. The new positive attitudes that he had helped the team espouse were beginning to restore Trimble to its former basketball glory.

The Tigers had bounced back from their loss to Randolph with four more wins, moving them to an 8–6 mark on the season with two more games remaining. The first of these two was to Randolph, who by the end of the season still managed to be undefeated. Despite a valiant effort by the Tigers, Randolph dealt Trimble its usual drubbing, 79–64. The point spread would have been even wider had Trimble not scored the last six points of the game against the Randolph subs.

However, if Trimble could just win its last game of the season—against South Side—it could finish in fourth place, behind Randolph, second-place Moraine, and third-place Roosevelt. That meant the Tigers might—just might—snare a spot in the finals.

As the day of the game approached, everyone on the Tiger team knew that in South Side, which had already beaten them once in early play, they were facing the biggest test of the year and of their young athletic lives.

More than their success on the court, Dyer was even happier about an important spiritual victory that the Tigers had scored just two days before the South Side game. One day during class-change, Miss Tanner, the journalism teacher, ran up to Coach Ramsbottom in the hall and waved him into her room.

"Coach, you won't believe it," Miss Tanner gasped as Ramsbottom made his way through what was now becoming a familiar line-up of desks. "For once, I have good news."

Her reporter, who had been following the drug case for more than two months now, had reported yesterday afternoon that the imminent drug connection involving some member of the basketball team had never materialized.

"All he was told was, 'The deal's off' No questions were asked; no questions were answered," said Miss Tanner. "But our reporter was convinced that the Trimble connection was a bad experience that the drug pusher wanted to forget."

Ramsbottom sighed enormously, then scowled.

"Great, but where does that leave us? Are you now going to go down to the principal's office and squeal, after having kept this under your hat for so long? Are you going to assume that our players are innocent until proven guilty? Or is this to be a matter just between you, me, and the reporter?"

"Now, Coach," consoled Miss Tanner, "you know I had only your best interests at heart. I hated to see your players get messed up with some bad business. As far as I'm concerned, it's a dead issue. There's nothing to report or write about. And I'll have to hand it to you. I don't know what you did or how you handled it, but I have the feeling that something you did saved our school a lot of embarrassment."

"I'm glad to know you think I can do something right," Ramsbottom replied sarcastically. "And now, if you'll excuse me, we have a game to play tonight. I'd like to save our school even more embarrassment on the court, if I can."

A much-relieved Ramsbottom had immediately telephoned Dyer with the good news. He said he thought it was appropriate that the minister, in keeping with past history, say a few words to the team just before they went on the court tonight in this all-important game with South Side.

So, on this quiet winter afternoon, as he surveyed the scene outdoors while mulling over the recent weeks, Dyer was making notes for his talk to the players.

Suddenly, there was a sharp knock at the door, and Reverend Lancaster entered the study, his face grim.

"John, my man, I have some bad news," he said.

"Good grief, what's wrong?" Dyer asked, startled out of his reverie by Lancaster's abruptness. "Did Mrs. Blackstone die?"

"No, it has nothing to do with someone's illness. Four hundred dollars has been discovered missing from Sunday's offering. It wasn't noticed until Monday when the money was recounted at the bank."

"Money missing? How can that be? Was there a break-in?"

"No, that's just it. Elmer Mundy, the president of the elders, put it in the church safe immediately after the Sunday service. The church safe was intact and there was no sign of vandalism."

"But that's preposterous," cried Dyer. "The only people who have keys are you, me, Elmer, and the janitor. Elmer has too much money to mess with that kind of small potatoes. He owns two feed mills here in town, and they're prospering quite well, I understand. Clinton Upton—why he's the only janitor this church has ever had. He takes care of this building better than someone would care for his own home. He's not well off, by any means, but if he were going to steal from the church, looks like he would have started stealing years ago. Besides, he and his wife both work. Their combined incomes should be adequate to take care of all their needs."

"I agree," said Lancaster, his eyes suddenly glued to the ground.

"Well, then what do you think?" Dyer probed, a little more anxiously now. "You have some clue you're not telling me about?"

Lancaster reddened, now speaking barely above a murmur.

"Well, I've been trying to avoid this, John, but I guess I'll have to lay the cards on the table. Some of the deacons and elders want you to meet with them on Wednesday to discuss this matter."

Dyer shot out of his chair, his fist clenched on the desk. "You can't be serious? You mean I'm a suspect in this? I can't believe it. Why would I take the money? Surely you've gotten something mixed up."

"Now, don't get excited," Lancaster warned. "Because you are new, they just don't know you as well as I do. They somehow have the idea that because you came here at a lower salary and you don't get your hair cut, you must somehow be in a position to need money. Now, just come to the meeting Wednesday and try to reconstruct yesterday's events in your mind as best you can. I'm sure you'll do just fine."

Dyer was suddenly enraged. "I won't go to that meeting and I won't be interrogated. It's just too much."

"Look, John, you have to go. Don't you see? Not to go would be the very worst thing imaginable. Surely something will turn up. We are all trying to figure out this mess. Until then, just keep your head—and things will be all right."

Lancaster ducked out the door quickly so he would not have to look any longer at Dyer's stunned face. Dyer stood motionless and for a moment stared blankly at the doorway where Lancaster had disappeared, then slumped back down into his chair to finish his notes. But he was angry and confused and, for the first time in his life, no words would come.

Over at Trimble, it was the most exciting afternoon at the school since the bomb threat happened two years ago.

Hardly a conversation occurred all day that did not center on tonight's game. Each teacher started off his or her class period with a cheer, "Beat the Southmen," and there was little concentration on the lesson after that. For the first time in years, the principal consented to allow the cheerleaders to stage a pep rally during the last period of the day.

The players were so hyped up that they hardly noticed that

Dyer had failed to make the pre-game talk that was becoming a tradition with the Tigers. Ramsbottom also had little to say, but merely paced up and down the dressing room, slapping players on the back as they passed him and looking nervously at his watch.

The game started slowly, with each team feeling the mounting pressure. After four minutes, the score was only 2–2. Then South Side moved ahead on a fast break and got the ball inside twice in a row against the Trimble man-to-man defense. The Tigers could answer with only a free throw. Ramsbottom took a time out and switched to a 2–3 zone, but South Side hit from the outside and led at the end of the quarter, 13–8.

The second quarter produced more of the same. Trimble was making a valiant effort, but nothing was working. Then, with 3:20 left in the half, trailing 24–16, the Tigers made their best charge. Freddie stole a cross-court pass and laid it up for two. Burns ripped off a rebound and got it out to Beck, who took it to the middle and hit Billy in the corner for an open shot which found the mark. Now the Tigers trailed by only four. The rest of the half, the two teams traded baskets and the half-time score ended in favor of South Side 36–32.

At half-time, Ramsbottom did not scold or cajole, as he had been known to do in former times, but quietly and deliberately went over a few of the mistakes that he had noticed. He advised the team to move into the middle of the defense more when their man did not have the ball, in order to shut off South Side's inside game more effectively.

But before letting them go out the door, he added as an afterthought, "Listen, there's no doubt in my mind that you are better players than South Side. And I believe you can win. When we meet here again, we'll either be in the play-offs, or it'll be all over until next year.

"But I just want you to know something. This has been one of the most memorable groups of players I have ever coached. You have come so far and accomplished so much in these few months, it's incredible. You've overcome lots of adversity and hard luck, and your attitudes have been just super. All day I've felt somehow that this was *our* game to-night—that we can do it, and that we ought to do it. So let's go out there and give it everything we've got."

The third quarter was one of the hardest-fought of the year. Both teams hustled the defense and banged the boards. Between the Tigers and the Southmen, they committed only three ball-handling errors in the entire quarter. But when it ended, South Side was still ahead by two, 54–52. Therefore, entering the fourth quarter—the part of the game that had often been so troublesome to them—the Tigers went in as the underdog.

South Side got the tip again, but speedy Joe Wilson stole the ball from the South Side ball-handler and broke away for two points to tie for the Tigers. Ramsbottom had decided to put Trimble in a full-court press every time they scored a point in the final quarter. It was his way of telling them that their hard work at the end of their practice sessions was going to give them the extra push it took to do well in the final quarter.

After Wilson's basket, the Tigers quickly formed their 2-2-1 zone press. The surprised South Side guard threw the ball directly into the hands of Freddie, and the Tigers took the lead for the first time in the game. The score was now 56–54. The Tiger fans picked up on the sudden surge of momentum and began to sound their battle cry, "Trimble, Trimble, Trimble! Make them quake, quake, quake!"

In the next three possessions, South Side failed to get the ball past the half line. Steals by Billy and Clark plus a ten-second violation gave the Tigers possession three times straight, and they converted with a field goal and two free throws by Billy and a two-pointer by Clark. The South Side coach went wild in frustration, waving his arms and demanding a time-out. The board read 62–54 in favor of Trimble—with 5:50 remaining on the clock. The stands were in a frenzy now, growing louder with every stanza of the yell.

In the huddle, Ramsbottom finally got enough order restored

to remind the players that they had a lot of time left and they would have to keep up the tough defense to get good shots. He closed with this reminder, "Remember your goal, and know that you have worked so hard that you have enough energy to play to midnight if you had to."

After the time-out, South Side settled down a bit and went into a more organized approach to get the ball up the floor, but still the Tiger defense prevailed. Trimble was falling back into a tough man-to-man when the ball got through the press. In the three minutes following the time-out, South Side could manage only five points on three free throws and a long-range field goal. In the meantime, Billy drove to the goal for three baskets, to capitalize on the fact that his man had four personal fouls. The last one was a three-point play that sent his defender to the bench with his fifth foul. Burns tipped in a shot missed by Freddie, and Beck hit on a short jumper, having come back in the game for Joe Wilson. With three minutes remaining, Trimble was up 73–59. South Side took its last time-out and moved into a desperation press of its own, immediately pressuring the Tigers into two errors—and Trimble's lead was cut to ten—73–63. Without hesitating further, Coach Ramsbottom took his final time-out to settle down his players.

"We are almost there now," said the coach, hardly concealing his excitement. "Just play with confidence and with all the strength you have in you. There is nothing to hold back for now; you have got to let everything go and allow yourselves to reach out and grab that goal. Meet their pressure with even more pressure of your own. And when you get the ball, make every shot be your own choice. Time is on your side. You are going to make it. You *ARE* going to make it."

Their faces bore the stamp of ironclad, unshakable determination as the Tigers broke out of the huddle.

"Clean those boards, Burnsie!" Billy cried.

"Stick to that defense, Freddie, Beck," yelled Symons.

"Let's do it now. Let's mop up," answered Burns.

And mop up they did. In the final three minutes, they put on an even better press than at the start of the fourth quarter. They completely crushed the South Side offense in outscoring them 16–3, allowing only three free throws those last three minutes. They executed a dazzling display of hard defense and rebounding against the taller South Side team. Good team spirit and teamwork had won the day.

As time ran out, the final score was Trimble 89, South Side 66. Pandemonium reigned on the court as the players carried off Ramsbottom on their shoulders for the first time that year. They had dreamed the impossible dream. The Tigers were play-off bound!

9

Tigers to the Defense!

It was mid-afternoon of the next day before Dyer's absence from the pre-game locker-room activities slowly began to dawn on Ramsbottom. The coach's daze was understandable, since the tension that permeated the locker room before the game was matched only by the pandemonium that reigned afterwards.

Virtually every resident of Trimble, from the mayor on down, stopped by that night on the way home from the gym to shake the hands and slap the backs of the coach and players.

Billy's parents, who quite amazingly had attended the past several games, surprised everyone—most of all Billy—by bringing in pizza and soft drinks as a victory celebration, and the team members gloried in recounting the play-by-play details of how they won the game.

The Williams' new involvement with Billy was another one of Dyer's victories. The minister had encouraged Billy to talk to his parents and tell them how much he needed their presence and support. However, the youngster had never been sure his remarks had been heard until his parents showed up with the refreshments that evening.

Although the victory over South Side merely ensured a play-off berth for Trimble, the noise that emerged from the dressing room sounded as though the Tigers had already taken the entire division title.

At about three o'clock on Saturday afternoon, when Ramsbottom at last sat down with a cup of coffee and began to relax a bit after a morning of unceasing congratulatory calls, he remembered that he had asked Dyer to stop by for his usual speech before the game. Not only had the minister failed to show, which was very unlike him, but Ramsbottom could not even remember Dyer being among the crowd of well-wishers who swamped the group later.

Just as he reached for the telephone to ring up the minister to see if something was wrong, the telephone buzzed and it was Dyer. "I've been trying to call you all morning, but from the busy signal I got, it sounded like other people had the same idea," Dyer began, trying to sound cheerful.

Quickly, then, with a great geyser of emotion, Dyer unloaded on Ramsbottom the details of the previous afternoon. He had been so distraught by the Reverend Lancaster's visit and the puzzling theft of which he was somehow suspect, that he had totally forgotten his promise to talk to the team.

"I guess you might say that for the first time in my life, I was speechless," said Dyer, trying desperately to bring the conversation back to a light tone. "But not only did I forget my speech, I forgot that I was even supposed to give one. I spent the evening sort of wandering aimlessly around my house, completely oblivious to the fact that there was a game in town. I guess it finally occurred to me sometime this morning, after a rather sleepless night. But from the looks of the final scoreboard, you did just fine without my pep talk. Congratulations, Coach. I'm proud of you. I knew you could do it."

But Ramsbottom refused to let Dyer change the subject.

"Forget about the game. Let's talk about you," the coach ordered. "What kind of preacher is Lancaster, coming at you with such an accusation? I've never heard of anything so ungrateful in my life. After all you've done for that church— bringing back people who haven't attended in years, getting all those young people active again, giving the place a much-needed breath of fresh air. And the very idea that a person of your moral caliber would steal even a penny. Why, I'm going over to the parsonage this very minute and give that preacher a piece of my mind."

"Coach, please," Dyer begged. "I'm touched by your concern. But, believe me, chewing out Lancaster would accomplish nothing. Besides, I'm telling you this story in confidence, because I felt I owed you an explanation about last night. I considered making up some wild tale. I could have told you that I was called away suddenly to visit a sick member, or that I had to attend a conference in another town. But I had to be up-front with you. You've been my biggest supporter since I've been in Trimble, and I've come to consider you as one of my best friends. Introducing me to your team has been one of the highlights of my life. I just couldn't live with a made-up tale."

"And that's exactly why I can't let you go through this alone, John," insisted Ramsbottom. "You've got it all wrong. You've been our team's biggest supporter. We couldn't have won that game last night, or any during the past several weeks, without your advice and your pep talks. You've helped us, and now we're going to help you. I've called a practice this afternoon at five and I'm going to tell the boys then. Or better yet, why don't you be there, and we'll tell them together. Eleven heads are certainly better than one. We'll put on our thinking caps and we'll help you tackle this thing head on."

"Coach, it seems so useless. The deck is stacked against me. There have been people in that church trying to set me up in something like this since I first came. I haven't been blind to it; I've just continued to hope that I could win them over. People have been jealous. They haven't taken too well to my long hair or my motorcycle. And my alliance with the team has angered them more. Looks like they might be looking for any excuse, even a trumped-up one, to make sure I don't stay very long."

"And we're not going to let them succeed," interjected Ramsbottom, using his military tones again. "Come on, John, where's the positive thinking that you taught us? Where's your spunk? Where's your drive? Better not let my players hear you talking in this hang-dog manner, or they'll think you don't practice what you preach. Now, John, I want you there at five this afternoon. This is a priority item. We're going to get busy and exonerate you from this. It's even more important than winning the play-offs."

Dyer managed a chuckle. "Now, Coach, I don't think you should go quite that far. But okay, if you insist, I'll be there. And thanks. Your concern for me really warms my heart."

But Ramsbottom, in his usual take-charge manner, did not wait for Dyer to arrive to tell the players. By the time the minister sputtered into the gym driveway on his motorcycle, the Tigers were already in a stew—and their practice to gear up for the play-offs was all but forgotten in light of Dyer's dreadful circumstances.

"Look, Reverend, I used to be the champion of my neighborhood in playing Clue," began Billy after everyone was seated. "Surely some of those detective skills paid off. I'll figure out this thing for you, I promise."

"Thanks, Billy, I'm sure you are quite a sleuth," the coach replied. "And we can use your help. But remember the team spirit that Reverend Dyer has taught us. We'll do a better job if we all work together."

Although visibly moved by the team's sympathy and support, Dyer was still hesitant to involve the youngsters in his problem.

"You must turn your full attention to winning in the play-offs," he cautioned. "If there ever was a time you should be single-minded, it's now. You need to concentrate on your goal cards more than ever, and figure out exactly what you can do individually and as a group to keep up the good work."

But the players, incensed that anyone would dare question the integrity of the man who had become their much-beloved mentor over the past weeks, refused to be daunted.

"Look, how about this plan?" suggested Freddie. "We'll divide into groups of two, and we'll talk to every member in the church if we have to, to see if we can't get a handle on this thing. Reverend, why don't you give us a list of the membership down at Union Church? We can start calling up people tonight. If each of us phones just seven or eight names a night, it won't take long at all."

"Great idea, and while we're at it, we'll kill two birds with one stone," chimed in Beck. "We'll tell the people of the church what a neat guy we think Reverend Dyer is. We'll lead a boycott there if they make him leave over this."

Dyer's eyes were brimming as he listened to the youngsters' conversation.

"Last night, I was beginning to wonder if I had a friend in the world," he said in a choked voice. "You folks have sure answered that question for me."

"You stuck by us when we were down," replied the coach. "Now we're going to stick by you and help bail you out of this thing."

Later that night, Billy tried to tell Sally about Dyer's dilemma when the couple went out for a pizza after practice.

"You just wouldn't believe the look on that guy's face," he said, obviously still caught up in the afternoon's events. "He looked the same way we felt the night after we lost to North Side early in the season. I can't believe such an awful thing could happen to him."

"He obviously means a lot to you," said Sally, with a hint of irritation in her voice.

Billy knew already that Sally was irked because they had

not gone out as much since Dyer first started wielding his influence over the team. In fact, Billy had asked Sally out for pizza that evening in hopes they could discuss their relationship and the direction it was headed.

At first, Sally had tried to blame Billy's absences on the fact that basketball and the Tigers' determination to earn a play-off spot were taking so much of Billy's time.

However, there was more to Billy's lack of attention lately than merely basketball. For one thing, he and his friends on the team had started going to church on Sundays, now that Dyer was drawing such a following from the young people. Since he was at church, Billy was no longer available to come to her house on Sunday mornings, which had been one of their regular times to be together. Over the years, Sally's parents had fallen into the habit of sleeping late on Sunday mornings instead of going to church, so they were often not even aware that Billy was in the house, or for how long.

"Yes, he does mean a lot to me, to answer your question," Billy finally replied. "Before Reverend Dyer started visiting the team, I didn't like myself very much. And because I didn't respect myself, I didn't respect other people either, including the other members of the team." He lowered his eyes and murmured, "And I think it may have even applied to you, Sally.

"I guess this doesn't sound too great. And maybe I shouldn't mention it at all. But we might as well be honest about our relationship. Before meeting the reverend, I looked on other people as things, as objects. The other players were just obstacles that got in the way of my achieving success. I couldn't see them as people, or as fellow team members. They were just objects, to be used to my advantage.

"In a way, I guess I felt the same about you. Maybe I wanted to date you for the wrong reason. Maybe I wanted to be seen with you for what you represented, for what you could add to my popularity. You're pretty and you're popular, and I guess I needed you for my ego.

"But I'm not comfortable with that anymore. I think about all the people who got abused in the process. There's poor Mrs. Hanna, the Spanish teacher. She was just a 'thing' to use for our amusement. We liked to razz her just to get her to react. And now."

Billy's voice trailed off on that note, as an immense pang of guilt enveloped him. Just this week, the students had learned that Mrs. Hanna had a husband who was critically ill with cancer. Expenses from his medical bills had been the reason that Mrs. Hanna had been forced to return to work this past fall, after a long absence from teaching. The strain of their financial situation, as well as the constant worry about her husband's health, had prevented her from being lighthearted and fun, as the students had wished. On the days that she seemed preoccupied and distant, she was almost sick with worry for having to leave her bedfast husband to come to school that day. Billy felt sick to his stomach to think about how the team members had added to her misery.

"And the same thing happened with poor Alice Smoots and Jump Otten," Billy said after a pause. "They were just toys for us to harass and then run off and leave. It was hard to think about them as part of God's creation. Fortunately, John Dyer taught us about forgiveness, too, or I'd never be able to live with myself."

One look at Sally's face told Billy that she hadn't tuned in to his monologue one bit.

"Oh, boy, isn't that just peachy?" she pouted. "Now I'm supposed to believe that I've been nothing to you all these months, except just an ornament, just someone to make you popular. So what am I supposed to think about all those times. Well, you know. You told me that you loved me, that we'd always be together. Does all that mean nothing to you?"

"I didn't say that," Billy replied. "I'm just questioning my motives, that's all. If we do love each other, it should be based on more than just physical need. It should be based on more than just my wanting to date the head cheerleader.

"But how about you? Weren't you far more interested in going out with the basketball star than with just plain old Billy? I don't think we ever stopped to think about plain old Billy or plain old Sally and what kinds of people we were underneath the glamour and the glitter. We were just going for the titles."

"Now you're trying to drag *me* into this," stormed Sally, her temper boiling. "This is sounding far too self-righteous to me. You're just riding high because you're in the play-offs, and you think you have a right to sound like Mr. Goody Two-Shoes. But what are you going to do when the bubble bursts, when you lose in the play-offs, and you're just plain old Billy Williams again? Do you think you'll still be singing the same song?"

"Maybe I will be just plain old Billy Williams," he replied. "And I'm sure I will be disappointed if we lose. But at least I'll still have my self-respect. I'll realize that I am somebody, regardless of whether I wear a basketball uniform. And that's more than I had when this season started.

"But look, Sally, we've argued enough. I didn't intend for this to turn into a shouting match. I have an idea. Why don't you just go to church with me on Sunday? Just one time won't hurt. You can see what Dyer is like, and you might just like him, too. It's a way for us to be together still. Besides, the suspense is building. We've got to catch the thief, and maybe by this Sunday we'll have his ears pinned back."

"That doesn't excite me one little bit," she retorted. "You can't make church sound exciting to me just by adding a little cloak-and-dagger routine. If you want to carry on about things like this, just remember, it's your loss. There are other fish in the sea. Now, please pay for the pizza and let's get out of here. I want you to take me home."

10

The Interrogation

Before John Dyer even had a chance to deliver a list of the church membership to Ramsbottom for the boys to begin their detective work, the minister was summoned to appear before the church board to talk about the missing funds.

Elmer Mundy, who called Dyer, said it was critical that the church act swiftly on the matter. He ordered Dyer to be at the Mundy home at eight that night, scarcely more than twenty-four hours after Reverend Lancaster first appeared in Dyer's office to announce the situation.

Dyer did not care for the tone of near-panic in Mundy's voice and did not understand why the meeting could not wait until the next day, when he would have had time to regain his composure and prepare his defense.

Even more insulting was the fact that Mundy announced he would "stop by" Dyer's apartment and escort him to the meeting. Dyer felt as if Mundy was beginning to treat him like some type of criminal, lurking in the shadows and waiting for the first chance to skip the country with the church's four hundred dollars.

When Dyer telephoned Ramsbottom to tell him of this latest development, the coach broke into one of his instant rages. "You can't go to that meeting by yourself, John," he stormed. "I'll go with you. You have to have someone there on your side. They'll turn this thing into a kangaroo court before your very eyes. I'll be over right this minute."

Dyer dissuaded him. "I'm afraid your presence will just inflame them more," he said. "If they're angry at me for spending time with the basketball players, you'll just be a further reminder of the things that they despise."

Mundy presided over Dyer's rushed-up trial as only a person of his stature as ruling lay leader of the congregation could do. His father and uncle had been lay leaders of Union Church before him, and Mundy held the old conservative views about everything in life. Peering through his thick glasses at the room that was packed with deacons, elders, Lancaster, and Dyer, Mundy read from a paper with a tone reminiscent of an executioner's reading of a prisoner's sentence.

"Gentlemen," he said with a loud clearing of his throat, "we are gathered here to discuss some business of the utmost urgency. As you know, we have a matter of some four hundred dollars missing from our offering last Sunday. After investigation in my capacity as chairman of this board and on the part of Reverend Lancaster, we have found it necessary to call before us Mr. John Dyer to give his account of the events of last Sunday. John, you have the floor."

Dyer chose to remain seated. "I'm afraid I don't quite understand what this is all about," he said. "All I can tell you is that I served during church services, and afterwards I stood in the vestibule and shook hands with people who were leaving the building. Immediately after that, I went home. There is nothing more to tell. Except, of course, that I had nothing to do with the money."

Mundy made no response to Dyer's statement, but instead charged forward with other remarks he seemed determined to make.

"Gentlemen, since this past Sunday, I have talked to many of the people of our church, and I have made a few phone calls to various places. As a result, I have compiled a long list of things for which I would like Mr. Dyer's response. Basically, Mr. Dyer, you have upset a goodly number of members of this church.

"First, there is the question of the money, which we'd like to pursue further with you. But second, in making these calls, we found out some things about you that you have been hiding from us. It was revealed that some years ago, before you studied at the seminary, you were employed as a slick advertising man with a prosperous Indianapolis firm and that you were making a huge salary—far more than you are now. You left that job and went to seminary, and that reduced your standard of living considerably. Now you drag around here with long hair that you rarely pay to have cut, and you owe money on that flashy motorcycle.

"To put it bluntly, Mr. Dyer, I'm sure that with these facts in hand, you can see why we would be questioning you in light of these missing funds. It seems that there are some details of your past that need explaining. So I turn the floor over to you, sir."

Dyer surveyed the fifteen pairs of eyes that were fixed on him and tried desperately to find at least a glimmer of warmth or sympathy or understanding behind someone's expression, but he saw only mistrust and hostility. He suddenly had an overwhelming urge to bolt for the nearest door and run out of the teeming room.

Instead, he took a deep breath as he stood and shook his head. "I suppose I could just give up and say that everything you say is true and hand in my resignation right here and now. I guess that would be the simplest way. But I am going to try a more difficult route—to answer your questions to your satisfaction.

"I can say truthfully that I have never been dishonest with you or tried to mislead you. When your pulpit committee contacted me about this job, no one ever questioned me about my life before seminary days. They were concerned only with my pastoral training and with my work in the ministry. My years in the ad agency were some time ago, and I never saw how my previous employment was important to anybody but me.

"But since the question has been raised, then I think you have a right to know. After I graduated from college, I did take a job with a big Indianapolis advertising concern. I did my job well and was promoted unbelievably fast. I quickly became an assistant vice-president and was in charge of advertising for the accounts of all the liquor distributors and distilleries that the company represented. I thought I was happy. I had a big car, a nice house with a pool, and a beautiful wife. I wore expensive suits to work every day. And believe it or not, I had my hair razor-cut every three weeks to where it never touched the tops of my ears or collar.

"Within ten years, I stood to be a very wealthy man if my progress continued. I was told that I had an amazing gift for being able to get people to do what I wanted, without having to force my wishes on them. Many told me I knew the words that would hit the largest number of people. Often, my wife and friends and boss told me how they found themselves changing their opinions about certain ideas after hearing mine. It wasn't something that I tried to force; it just happened. My boss told me that I had a sparkling future with the company.

"But, one day, my wife was driving home from the city to the suburbs where we lived. As she went through an intersection on the green signal, a drunk driver ran through a red light and struck her car. She lived in intensive care for three days, and then it was over.

"After the shock of her death wore off, I went over these events in my mind a thousand times. I remembered what she and my boss had told me about my persuasiveness. I dismissed the guilt as best as I could, but I decided that if I had any power at all to influence people's minds, I would *not* use it to convince them to drink a specific kind of alcohol.

"When I turned in my resignation to Mr. White, my boss, and told him I was leaving to enter the seminary, he did not blow up in rage as I had feared. He told me that although he was not a religious man, he could see why the ministry was an ideal field for me. He said something like this: 'Advertising makes a living by measuring the feelings, wants, and attitudes of the other person. Those in advertising who have succeeded the best are those who have learned to apply the idea of loving another as they love themselves. A man who is at war with himself thinks that everyone else must be his enemy as well. If you believe in yourself, then you believe in the next man—and when you believe in him, then you can assess his needs correctly. And these principles work in the ministry as well as they do in advertising. I'll hate to lose you, John, but I know you'll do well.'

"His words convinced me that the church was a more appropriate outlet for my talents. So I finished the seminary in two years instead of the usual three, and I was on the staff of the church in suburban Indianapolis before coming here.

"It's true, if I were still in advertising, I'd be making three or four times my income at Union Church. But I wouldn't be happy. Since I've been your minister, I have felt that at last I was in the spot that God had in mind for me. I know that my motorcycle and my long hair have been a turn-off for some of you. After spending the first four years of my career looking conventional and driving fancy cars and wearing suits, I decided that I never wanted to be part of that scene again. I began dressing this way and riding my Yamaha because I felt it would help me relate to young people.

"Well, that's all I have to say. I hope you decide in my favor. But regardless of your final verdict, I just want you to know that the six months during which I've been your assistant minister have been the most fulfilling of my life. And if I wanted or needed more money, I'd have quit my job here and gone back into advertising, instead of stealing from the church."

As Dyer sat down, the room was hushed. Finally, Mundy rose and said, "I am going to ask you to leave the room now, while we discuss these matters." Instead of watching him leave, the fifteen pairs of eyes turned downward while Dyer moved toward the door.

Once the door closed behind Dyer, Mundy continued, "Gentlemen, as for me, I was moved by the young man's story. I truly don't believe he took the money. He left his old job in good standing. I actually talked to his old boss, Mr. White. He confirmed that he was a good worker, and said he'd hire him back in a minute. And I'm sure Dyer is right—he would have left this church long ago and gone right back into his old field if he had been desperate for cash. Without a wife and family, and with his parsonage allowance to help pay the rent, I'm sure he can swing the monthly note on that motorcycle with little problem. And goodness knows, he doesn't spend any money on clothes or grooming—we can all see that—although I can see why that seems unimportant to him.

"But we've got money missing and we still don't know who took it. Until we answer that question, I'm afraid Dyer will have to continue to be our prime suspect. He's the only person in the whole church who is a stranger in our midst."

Then Frank Fender came forward to speak, a rare occurrence since he was nearing eighty and was hard of hearing. A retired minister and an emeritus member of the board, Fender was invited to these functions merely as an obligatory gesture in respect for his past years of service. During most meetings, Fender sat in one corner and nodded in sleep as business was conducted.

"My friends, I have been a believer for some seventy years,

and I have seen a lot of people come and go at this church in my time," he said. "In my opinion, you would be making the mistake of your lives to turn this young man out. Last week they gave us old folks his former Sunday School room because his class had become so large that they had to move out to bigger quarters. I haven't seen so many young people in the church in all my life. There ought to be some kind of a lesson there in itself."

As Fender shuffled to his seat and sat down, Lancaster spoke up. "The truth is, John Dyer has helped me, too. He has helped me to see my work in a positive way. You know, being a minister isn't always the most cheerful job in the world. Few people come to talk with you when they're feeling good— just when they're feeling bad. But working around John has made me appreciate even the menial things I do. He has helped me view all the complaints and gripes I hear as a vital part of my ministry. I certainly can't feel right about letting him go. We must clear up this money issue and give him a chance to continue."

Several other heads nodded in assent. Mundy said, "I'm still perplexed by this whole thing, but if it is your consensus that we should wipe the slate clean with Dyer, so be it. Reverend Lancaster, go to Mr. Dyer and tell him to treat the matter as though it had never happened."

But the damage was already done. The insinuations, the doubts, the hostility, the rushed-up trial, the interrogations— they all had a chilling effect on Dyer. Sitting in a deserted pew in the darkened sanctuary while the ruling leaders of Union Church debated his fate, Dyer determined that whatever their ruling, he would announce his resignation at the regular services the following Sunday.

11

Super Sleuths

The next few days were a blur of activity for the Trimble Tigers. The team members were so busy interviewing members of Union Church about the missing money that they scarcely had time to become nervous about the crucial play-off game coming up that week with Moraine.

On the morning after the "trial," a downcast Dyer had called Ramsbottom to tell him of his decision to resign. Instead of replying with outrage, Ramsbottom merely acted as though he had not heard Dyer's remark. He announced that he would be at Dyer's house within ten minutes to pick up the list, so that the boys could begin their work immediately after school that day.

The players went on a rampage, genuinely enjoying the challenge of the detective hunt, while hoping to clear Dyer's name of suspicion. Many of the church members were taken aback by the boldness of their calls, and were doubly shocked that the Trimble High basketball players would undertake such a project in the first place.

For instance, Beck rode his new Honda, that he had acquired by earning money in Mr. Symons's store, to call on Joe Chaney, the hardware-store manager, who was a longtime Sunday school teacher at Union Church.

When Beck told Chaney the purpose of his visit, the man replied, "My goodness, why aren't you boys down at the gym practicing, instead of out socializing like this? It seems like a strange use of your time for a team that has a title game coming up soon."

Nevertheless, the players felt they could sense a few hardened hearts soften toward Dyer after only a few minutes of conversation.

When Freddie told Mrs. Pomeroy, president of the ladies' missionary society, how much Dyer's friendship had meant to him personally, she replied, "You know, I never cared much for that new minister before. But I can remember what you were like just nine months ago, and you weren't the type of youngster I cared to have coming to the church house. So I guess if the reverend can make a new creature out of you, he must be worth paying some mind to."

However, although they spent many hours giving pep talks for Dyer—as well as answering many questions about the upcoming Moraine game—the boys emerged after five days of calls without any serious leads about the missing funds.

Ramsbottom at first was secretly worried that the investigation would take too much time away from practice. So he was pleasantly surprised that the boys seemed to have more energy than ever at their drills and worked better together than before. The camaraderie that was necessary to plot out their research plan for Dyer was translating into an even greater team spirit than the Tigers had known before the victory over South Side.

But, after they had worked for five days without any answers, Ramsbottom regretfully told the boys they must put their detective work on the back burner for the next few days—until after the Moraine game was over.

Practices went smoothly, and the Tigers were gunning for Moraine, the team that had finished right behind Randolph in the final standings. During the regular season, the Tigers had split with Moraine, each winning on their respective home courts. Moraine had won 71–69 early in the year, and then Trimble avenged the loss with a score of 80–64 near the end of the season. Everyone had a lot of confidence that the Tigers' successes would continue in this important game, which was being played on the neutral South Side court.

However, the day before the game, the Tigers received some disturbing news. Billy did not come to school in the morning because he was in bed with a fever from some kind of virus, according to the doctor. It was doubtful that he would be able to play against Moraine on Saturday.

Ramsbottom did the best he could to adjust the offense and the game plan to allow for Billy's absence—inserting Bobby Prentice into the line-up. Still, without the twenty points and ten rebounds that Billy could be expected to produce in an average game, it would be a difficult job to beat Moraine under these circumstances.

At Saturday noon, the doctor told Ramsbottom and Billy's parents that Billy could play one quarter and that was all. Coach Ramsbottom decided he would save Billy for the last quarter. Or, if things worked out that he did not have to play Billy at all, he would hold the boy out the entire game, so he could save his strength for the championship game the following week.

The South Side gym was running over with screaming, expectant fans on a cold but clear February night. Freddie and Beck were lined up against Moraine's fiery little guards, Mickey Marlowe and Ronnie Mayo. Burns would jump center against big Eddie Ernst, at 6'9", the tallest man in the league. The forwards, Clark and Bobby, would try to handle Moraine's Carl Roberts and Fred Jennings.

Although the Moraine forwards were not as effective as their guards or the big man, they had the extra advantage of having Eddie Ernst behind them. Since the defense had to pay a lot of attention to Ernst, it allowed the forwards to get open more easily than they would have been able to on their own. It was going to be a tough game.

Moraine had not known that Billy would not be in the lineup and had directed their pre-game strategy toward Billy, both on offense and defense. When they saw that he would not be in the game, they suffered a bit of a psychological letdown while the fired-up Tigers roared out to a surprising 14–6 lead. Ironically, Bobby, who was subbing for Billy, had scored six points to lead the way.

After a Moraine time-out, Trimble kept pumping the adrenalin and putting on the pressure. Although the Moraine backcourt was regarded as the top duo in the circuit, Beck and Freddie for the Tigers worked like two parts of the same body as they helped each other on defense. They limited the Moraine pair to four points the first half and stole the ball from them a total of five times, turning their efforts into Tiger baskets. Through their ball-hawking and fast breaks, they managed to split twenty points right down the middle by half-time. As the teams headed for the locker room, the board read Trimble 42, Moraine 35.

During the first half, the Tiger bench had been alive, including Billy, who forgot about his sore throat and was doing all he could to lend enthusiasm. Ramsbottom, who noticed Billy out of the corner of his eye, could not help but remember the jealous, threatened player of only a few months ago. He marveled that Billy could be so eager for his team without being in the limelight.

However, early in the third quarter, the momentum changed, and the Tigers found less to yell about. The Indians had suddenly realized that they had a real game on their hands, even with Williams on the bench. Ernst tipped to the side and the speedy Moraine guards broke loose for a quick two-pointer. As play continued, the guards tried to set the big center up and he went to work against Burns. Both Symons and Prentice tried to give Burns some help on the big man, but he overpowered them all. With one minute to go in the third quarter, Burns picked up his fourth foul. Ernst connected on both ends of the free throw to put the Indians ahead for the first time in the game, 59–57. At a time-out, Ramsbottom decided to put the Tigers in a 2–3 zone to help protect Burns from fouling out. The coach was going with Burns, even with four fouls.

The change to zone helped for the final minute of the quarter, as Moraine failed to adjust its offense immediately, and Trimble grabbed the lead back by a point at the quarter stop. It was then Trimble 62, Moraine 61.

Ramsbottom approached his benched player. "How do you feel, Billy?" he asked. "Do you have the energy to play?"

"I want to try it, Coach. I think I can do it," he replied.

"Okay. You check in for Burns and go as hard as you can for two or three minutes. We'll get Burns in for you when you tire, and then we can go from there. You play in the middle of the zone and stay in front of Ernst all the time. Bobby, you and Clark have to fill in behind Ernst when the ball is on the side of the floor opposite you. There is no way we can let Billy play behind that big stick and expect to stop him. We have to rely on Billy's quickness and on you guys being alert enough to give help if they try to lob the ball over his head."

The Tigers got an immediate lift from the presence of Billy in the game. Ramsbottom's strategy was working well. Moraine continued to try to feed Ernst, but when he did get the ball, he had to come away from under the goal and was not effective. Twice they tried to lob over the top, and Symons knocked one pass out of bounds and stole the second. On the Tiger end of the floor, the Moraine defense focused on Billy as they had practiced.

But Billy, now playing more as a team man, fed inside to Symons twice and pitched off once each to the Tiger pair of guards for baskets. After three minutes and forty seconds of play, Burns was standing at the score bench, waiting to check in for Billy, as the coach had promised.

All the players grabbed Billy as he came off the floor, exhausted and flushed—but ebullient. The board read 72–62. Although Billy had not scored a point, he had turned the game around. The Tigers held on to win, 84–77.

It was all set. In the same evening, Randolph trounced Roosevelt, 89–62, to pick up the team's seventeenth consecutive win of the season. The following Saturday would be the championship game on the Central High floor—between Trimble and Randolph.

12

The Top of the Mountain

Time seemed to stand still in the next two days as the incredulous Tigers prepared for their monumental game with Randolph.

No one in school—least of all the Tigers themselves—could actually believe that their team, which had begun the year with such a bleak, unpromising start—was now vying for the championship with the only undefeated school in the league.

In all their years of playing basketball—even last season when they easily won the district championship without much effort—Freddie, Billy, and Beck, the head triumvirate of the Tiger team, had never known such excitement, and that spirit permeated the entire student body.

The teachers were just as caught up in the frenzy and seemed not to mind that many of their pupils hardly listened to a single word in class the day before the final match. Even serious Mrs. Hanna, despite her growing preoccupation with her husband's illness, had thrown her support behind the team. On the day after the victory over Moraine, she had immediately arranged a party for the class on Friday and had postponed the Spanish exam until after the championship game. Although she had not been at school all week because her husband had suffered a relapse, she had arranged for a substitute to stop by the bakery on the square to pick up the cookies and make sure that the party came off on schedule.

The only cloud over the whole jubilation continued to be the Tigers' concern for John Dyer and his troubles at Union Church. The players had persisted in making their contacts. Freddie and Billy were even late to class on the morning after the Moraine game, just so they could telephone their quota of ten Union church members whom they had postponed calling the night before while they were on the court.

Ramsbottom was unabashedly proud that these youngsters, who might otherwise have been on an ego trip about their victory, were more concerned with working to clear their friend's name.

Ramsbottom commended Freddie about this when he saw the student in the hall between classes. "I'm really proud of you, son. That's the mark of a great man, you know—putting other people above yourself," he said.

"Oh, that's okay, Coach; I'm just sorry nothing has material-ized to help John Dyer yet. But I did learn an interesting bit of gossip this morning that intrigued me a lot."

"Really? What's that?" Ramsbottom questioned.

"Well, I was interviewing Mrs. McCormick. She's been a member of Union Church practically since she was a baby, and her parents were some of the founding members a long time ago. Anyway, I told her what we were doing, interviewing people, and she said, 'I don't know why you're so concerned. That's what our church gets for hiring these outsiders instead of sticking to people in the church who are capable of filling the pulpit.'

"I asked her who she meant, and she said people like Clinton

Upton. I guess I must have had a funny look on my face. I mean, the church janitor? Could someone really think he'd make a good preacher?

" 'Well,' she said, 'didn't you know? Clinton Upton studied for the ministry once.' She told me he even took some classes at a seminary. Except he never preached a lick. Too scared to go up in front of a group. She said some folks think he's got a mental block about speaking. That's why he sweeps the floors instead of teaching Sunday school. He apparently gets tongue-tied talking to more than one person at a time.

"What a funny place that church is. A janitor who used to be a preacher. Oh, well, gotta go, Coach. See you this afternoon."

When Dyer called that afternoon to congratulate the coach on the previous night's win, Ramsbottom merely mentioned in passing the bit of gossip that Freddie had told him that day.

"It's almost too ridiculous to talk about," Ramsbottom said, prefacing his remarks.

But Dyer seized on every detail with great interest.

"He's the only janitor the church has ever had in recent years," mused Dyer. "He moved over from the old building and has been here through three ministers. Clinton probably feels that this church belongs to him more than anyone else, and sometimes he treats others almost like trespassers. But no one ever gets angry at him because he takes care of the building better than a man would take care of his own home.

"His main job is at the lumberyard, cutting and loading the wood in the warehouse, but he comes to the church every Saturday and does many extra maintenance chores for only about a hundred dollars a month. Not that he needs that. I know he gives it all back in the offering. He and his wife spend practically nothing on themselves. They both have jobs and they have no children to support. If he once studied for the ministry, he may feel guilty for not pursuing it and think he must make it up to the church by being the person who cleans—and for nothing."

Ramsbottom was silent, pondering Dyer's remarks, so the minister went on: "Clinton was one of the four people who had the key to the safe. But he certainly doesn't need the money, and he's the last person in the world who would want to do the church harm. In many ways, it's his whole life."

"Maybe he wouldn't want to do the church harm, but what about doing harm to you?" Ramsbottom ventured. "If he's always wanted to be a preacher, he may hold real animosity toward anyone in that role, especially someone as poised and successful as you are, who came in from the outside."

"I don't know, Coach," said Dyer, growing very somber. "It's a puzzling matter, a very puzzling matter," he said, his voice trailing off.

Then he suddenly snapped back to the moment. "But, Coach, don't you go worrying about it any more than you have already. You have a championship to win. Now hang up the phone this minute and get to the practice with your boys."

At Ramsbottom's request, Dyer made a brief appearance on Friday night in the locker room, just before the boys went on the court for the championship game.

Ramsbottom introduced Dyer as "the man who turned our world around for us this year." As he stood, the boys went wild with supportive applause.

"I'll say to you something similar to what I mentioned to you the first time I came," said Dyer when the clapping ceased. "That is, *I* didn't score a point, grab a rebound, or block a shot this season. What you have done, you have done together. If I helped you to realize fully the potential you all have within you, I am glad for it. But, in truth, you already had the ability, and with good practice and by developing a new attitude, you did it all yourselves. Remember that you only did in basketball what you are capable of doing in any area of your lives in the future. Whether or not you become champions tonight, you have tried to seek the best in yourselves, and that is the winning thing to do."

Billy raised his hand. "You know, Reverend Dyer, when you first came to visit us, I didn't want to listen, because I was afraid you'd talk only about religion and quote a lot of Bible verses to us. Well, you didn't mention religion at all, even though what you had to say made a lot of sense."

Dyer replied, "I know what you mean, in that I didn't refer to the Bible or to the traditional topics of sermons. But, in my opinion, everything I said was of a religious nature. Because to me, anyway, religion involves a change of attitude. When you change your attitude to one that exhibits love of God or of self and of others, you have covered a lot.

"When you have set goals and take time to relax and control the thoughts you put into your mind, you can change your whole life around. This is true in basketball and in everything else. When you learn to think about the creative ideas you want to fulfill, take time to rehearse them on the screen in your mind. Then carry out your best efforts with love and forgiveness in your heart, to realize the best that is in you. It seems to me that God showed us the best way to do that, but I think everyone can use these truths, whether or not they call themselves religious.

"I wish you the very best for your game tonight, and for the game of life we are all destined to play."

The starting lineups were the same for both teams as they had been for the first two games against Randolph. It was Freddie and Beck at guard against Lionel Sanders and Jeep Scott. Curtis Burns would jump against Arnie Aldrich, while Billy and Clark would battle against Randolph's big forwards—Jeff Black and Scott Bragg.

The Central High gym was more than filled; people were standing in the aisles and doorways. During the warm-ups, excitement electrified the entire gymnasium, as the drama of young men putting everything on the line unfolded. The cheering sections took turns trying to out-yell each other, and the crowd members on both sides were hoarse before the game even began. The scene was frantic.

The first quarter ended tied at 14–14. Each team was playing it close to the belt, and good shots were at a premium. The second quarter was much the same as the first. Both teams stayed with their man-to-man defenses and fiercely battled each other. It was still tied at the half—32–32.

As the third quarter began, Billy was called for a charge, his third foul. He had already scored eleven points and had held Scott Bragg, the Pirates' leading scorer, to one field goal and two free throws. Coach Ramsbottom wanted to keep Billy in the game because it was so tight, but within a minute, Billy had committed his fourth foul on a rebound. The score was Trimble 40, Randolph 37. Bobby Prentice entered the game for dejected Billy. While Bobby was a good sub, he was shorter than Billy, who was already smaller than his man, Scott Bragg. The difference proved to be too much. Changing Clark Symons to guard Bragg did not help. The whole Tiger game sagged, and the third quarter ended with Randolph on top by five, 59–54.

Ramsbottom faced a tough decision. Should he go with Billy now—or wait? He elected to wait to see if things got worse. It was a reasonable decision, but things got worse sooner than he expected. With 6:17 showing on the clock, the Pirates had hammered ahead, 69–60. To get Billy back into the game, the coach called a time-out and instructed the team to go the full-court press and fall back into a zone at the half-court area. Billy was told to play the best that he could without fouling. The coach admonished the players, "You have time and you have the strength. You can press them right out of this. You are quicker and you want it. Now go get it."

The Tigers scored on their first play and cut the lead to

seven. Randolph guard Jeep Scott tried to throw long to Aldrich to beat the press, but Burns came down with the ball. He threw to Symons who then fed Billy cutting into the middle, and the lead was down to five. For the next four minutes, the lead changed from three to five to seven and back to five again.

Then, with 1:50 remaining in the game, Symons stole the ball from Jeff Black and got it to Freddie in the middle of the court. Freddie and Beck went two-on-two against the Randolph guards. Beck took the shot on the right side and banked it in just as he was hit by Lionel Sanders. Beck made good the free throw and the score stood at 81–79, Randolph's favor.

Randolph took a time-out and went into a stall, trying to draw the Tiger defense out on the floor for a foul or for an easy opening behind the defense. Ramsbottom had expected this move, and had told the defense to let Freddie, Beck, and Symons chase the ball out front and try to get possession without fouling. Billy would stay in the foul-line area, while Burns would guard the basket in order to prevent any lay-up.

As the ball came in bounds, the Randolph guards moved the ball around in the deep area near the half line. The clock ran down to 1:10, and then the referee called traveling against Randolph's Jeep Scott. Trimble had the ball, only two points down.

Freddie was determined to get the ball to Billy, figuring this was the best chance they had to score. Just as Billy received the pass and started his drive to the basket, he saw Symons open near the goal. As desperately as Billy wanted this tying shot, he fired the pass to Symons, who seemed within easy reach. Symons went up and missed it. But Burns came in running with his most aggressive jump of the season and tipped the shot in. The game was tied.

Randolph took another time-out with forty seconds showing on the clock. Ramsbottom told his team in the time-out that he wanted to shift to the man-to-man press and do everything except foul to steal the in-bounds pass. "Whatever you do, just make sure your man doesn't get the ball in bounds," he ordered.

Randolph was not quite ready for this change in defense. Scott held the ball out of bounds while his teammates tried to get open. They could not shake the Tiger defense. The whistle blew and amid the pandemonium the referee signaled five seconds and handed the ball to the Tigers. The Tigers took a time-out and Ramsbottom shouted for the team to work the ball outside until ten seconds showed on the clock, and then to run their back-door play for Freddie.

"They will be looking for Billy to get the ball, but he is the decoy," Ramsbottom told them. "Billy will break up high, pulling the defense. The pass will instead go to Symons, busting up into the circle. Beck will throw to Symons and he will feed Freddie going to the goal. If that's not open, Beck will go one-on-one to the goal."

With fifteen seconds left, Freddie signaled for everyone to get organized, and the play began. Everything worked except for the basket. Freddie got clobbered as he tried to lay it in and had to go to the line for two shots. There were six seconds showing on the clock.

Freddie had improved as a foul-shooter, but he was not yet a great one at the line. Tension grabbed the entire crowd as Freddie went to the stripe. He put the first one in the air, and it rolled around and dropped through the net. The Tigers had the lead by one point.

The second shot hit the front of the rim, then the back, and bounded out. In the battle for the rebound, the ball was knocked to near mid-court. Beck and Freddie went for it, but speedy little Jeep Scott of Randolph nabbed the ball away from them with three seconds left. He flipped the ball to Scott Bragg, who picked it up as it rolled near the mid-line and let the ball fly toward the basket. The horn sounded just as the basketball bounced off the Randolph backboard and rim.

It was over. The Tigers were champs. Randolph had been beaten, 82–81.

Instead of the clamor that might be expected to emerge from the Trimble dressing room after such an event, the Tigers were unusually subdued. They had made a long, tough journey and had reached the top. The players felt as though they were walking in a dream. Nobody thought to shower or get dressed. Players merely walked around, staring at each other in disbelief.

Ramsbottom instantly sized up the situation and seized the moment: "We believed enough to reach for the top," he said to the group who gathered around him. "We dared to set this goal, even though it seemed impossible because of the way we began the year. We did it because we had the courage to reach for the highest. We played hard and we won it. I think each of us has learned that from now on we can all reach for the top. And even if you never quite make it, the view is still much better near the top of the mountain than it is in the caverns below. Now let's have a moment of silent, thankful prayer before we celebrate further."

Everyone understood.

The noise outside the hushed Tiger locker room indicated that the celebration had already begun for the rest of the town. And, truly, it did seem that all 20,000 inhabitants of Trimble were packed into the crowded gym, squealing and yelling at the tops of their lungs.

But at least one Trimble basketball fan had skipped out early and was missing the celebration.

John Dyer was not part of the victorious cheering scene. He had left as the final buzzer sounded and was at that moment knocking on the door of Clinton Upton.

13

A Parting Shot

The white bungalow with the brown trim, where Clinton Upton and his wife had lived for all of their forty years of marriage, looked as if it belonged to a man who was content to live without the luxuries of life.

As Dyer knocked on the door and Upton's wife admitted him to the living room, the minister could not help noticing the extremely spartan furnishings. A car which Dyer could recognize as being a model at least twenty years old was parked in the driveway, and Dyer was sure that the television that stood next to the door in the living room was one of the first models ever manufactured.

Dyer had been prompted to make this late-night call on Upton because he had been haunted by the very words that he uttered to the Tigers during his pre-game speech to them: "When you have set goals—when you think about the ideas you want to fulfill, when you take time to rehearse them on the screen in your mind and carry out your best efforts with love and forgiveness in your heart, you can realize the best that is in you."

In the past few days, as the conflict over the missing funds had come to a head, Dyer realized that he had actually begun thinking of himself as a loser. He had talked a good game to the boys, he realized, but he had failed to practice what he preached. The goals and ideas that he wanted to fulfill at Union Church had been quickly eroded by his befuddlement about his own situation.

Instead of rolling over and playing dead and letting a few church members run him out from a job he adored, Dyer decided while sitting in the midst of the cheering crowd at the gym that he would make one final stab at making some sense of this mystery. It was a long shot—a very long shot—but perhaps Clinton Upton held the answer.

After what seemed like an eternity since Dyer was ushered in, Upton appeared, staring mainly at his feet as he offered Dyer an unenthusiastic handshake and muttered almost inaudibly for the minister to sit down. As they sat, Upton continued to avoid eye contact with Dyer and obviously had no plans for making small talk, for he said nothing. So Dyer decided to plunge right in with his speech.

"Clinton, I apologize for barging in so late, but I had to tell you about a decision I've made. You're the very first person I've told about this," Dyer began. "I've decided to resign at the church on Sunday. There's been too much doubt, too many suspicions, too many accusations, for me to continue to work effectively. I'm still young, and I still have some contacts in the advertising field. I can go back to Indianapolis and try to make a new life for myself in my old profession."

Upton looked up sharply, suddenly startled by Dyer's remarks. "Why would you do that?" he asked, speaking above a murmur for the first time. "I know what happened at the board meeting this week. Heard folks talking about it when I cleaned up later. They asked you to forget everything that happened."

"That's true. They did, and I'm grateful for that," Dyer

said. "But the young people of the church need someone whom everyone considers above reproach. I feel as though I can no longer be a good example to them, and that this cloud will continue to hang over me as long as I remain here.

"But that's really not why I'm here to talk to you. Truth is, I must be really behind the times. Do you know that I learned just yesterday that you once wanted to be a minister? That you even took some seminary courses to prepare you for the pulpit? I don't mean to embarrass you, but is this really true?"

"Correct," Upton replied tersely, looking down at his feet again.

"Well, I'm glad you told me. It's a shame for you to have that training and that desire and not use it. Would you mind telling me why you never followed through with your plans?"

"Nobody's business, really," said Upton, growing belligerent.

"You're probably right. I'm meddling by talking about it," Dyer replied. "But somehow, I just wondered if it is because talking before groups turned you off. Because if it is, I just couldn't leave town without sharing a little of myself with you. It may surprise you, but I had the same hang-up many years ago, before I was in the ministry. I could be a good salesman for a product or for an idea, when I was working one-to-one in advertising. But when I got around bunches of folks, I just froze. I knew that if I wanted to preach, I'd have to do better. I'll tell you what worked for me, in hopes that it might help you, too."

Upton still stared at the ground, but the expression on his face indicated he was listening.

"Get alone somewhere and close your eyes," continued Dyer. "Draw a blank screen in your mind as if in a movie theater and picture yourself getting up before a church group to speak. Now try to visualize the very worst things happening while you are up there trying to talk.

"First you imagine that you can't get any sound at all. Then your voice squeaks. Then people laugh at you; maybe they throw vegetables at you. Feel yourself being as embarrassed as you can be. Repeat those pictures over and over in your mind for a few minutes until you can flash those pictures on the screen without feeling much response inside.

"Then, after you have done that, draw a new screen and put yourself on it again. This time tell yourself that you have something so important to say that it doesn't matter what people say or do, that you are going to say it anyway. Think that you have talked to hostile groups before, you have made mistakes before, and you have been embarrassed before. But none of this matters now in your new vision—because you have something so terribly vital to say that you will say it with all your strength. Then see yourself successfully saying what you want to say. Repeat that as long as it takes, and never let those bad pictures in again.

"Clinton, you have to repeat this process a lot of times before you are able to stand before a group and speak. You will have to do it occasionally afterwards in order to keep you going once you get started. But if you will believe that God has actually given you the power to do this thing, you will be able to do it. I promise you. It worked for me and helped me overcome my fears. I know it can help you, too.

"I just want you to know that wherever I go, I'll pray for you that you will conquer this need, because I know that being able to recognize this dream will make your life richer. If I don't see you again, I wish you the very best."

Upton said nothing, but merely nodded as Dyer finished his remarks. Dyer stood to go, shook Upton's hand, and uttered a brief good-bye.

Dyer had tried everything he could think of to do. He had thought that if Upton had any knowledge about the mysterious disappearance of the church funds, he would have surely spoken up during the discussion. Perhaps he had been wrong to visit the man at his home; perhaps his words had been too offensive and would cause the man to withdraw even more. But at least Dyer could leave town knowing that his conscience was clear.

"Whether or not you become champions tonight, you have tried to seek the best that is in you, and that is the winning thing to do," he had told the Tigers in his pre-game remarks.

Dyer believed that his visit to Upton had qualified on both scores: He had tried to seek the truth from the janitor, not by accusing or insinuating, as the church board had dealt with him, but in a more honorable way—by helping the man to realize the potential in himself and thus showing him how to get in touch with his feelings about his own capabilities. In so doing, even though Upton had not come forth with the answer that Dyer had hoped for, the minister could still go out thinking of himself as a winner.

14

Victors All

Sunday morning arrived far too quickly. Dyer was determined to make it through his Sunday school lesson without even a hint of the speech he would give at the close of the service.

However, since he felt this would be the last Sunday he would ever speak to the group, Dyer wanted to make sure every word counted. He wanted to be certain that he told the group everything that had been on his heart for the past six months.

He began his talk by saying, "Many of you have told me that religious matters have turned you off at times. Perhaps that is because occasionally those who teach these lessons concentrate too heavily on the fearful or negative aspects of life. Today let us concentrate on the positive benefits of belief, in hopes of finding some help for our lives today.

"There are a lot of good reasons why a person should come to believe and to allow that belief to affect his life in a positive way. Certainly there are ideas and events we must take stands against—crimes, injustice, inhumanity. But effective living must be directed toward goals and worthy ideas, not simply against evil.

"Living effectively is basically seeking to live up to the best of your potential as you see it, attempting to live in such a way that you can respect yourself and give love to others. You must make this a personal journey and know that you will make some errors along the way. But when the one who begins the journey knows about God's forgiveness, he must practice forgiving himself as he makes an honest effort at living his best.

"Man is important as the peak of all creation. But to arrive at his best, he needs to get in harmony so that his acts are attune to what he feels in his heart. It doesn't work to do things because you are impressed with me or some other person, or because you are scared to death, or because your parents will be pleased, or even for the sake of the rules of society. People who follow only the outside pressures are not being themselves. In my opinion, the point at which a person becomes himself and when his decisions really begin to count is when he takes time to examine his decisions and comes to a moment when he says to himself, 'I believe this. This is me.' It's not that a person is free to do whatever he desires or feels without carrying a big responsibility. Our feelings and desires can be very misleading. But, in the end, rewards are greater, I believe, for the man who tries to live from within than for the person who is always trying to please others.

"Naturally, it is easier to float through life and not give these notions a thought. It is far easier to follow others' values and rules. It's simpler never to commit yourself to anything or anyone.

"But to neglect these decisions and take the easy course is to suffer through life as a wanderer, because you will have failed to do the one thing you were created for; the one thing no other person in the world can do—to become the 'best you.'

"So, how do we do it? Just as we have mentioned before, when we decide on a goal or course of action, we must use the tools of thought control to aid our progress. Submit your goals or ideals to a piece of paper. Then take time to relax and review these on the screen of your mind. Over and over, see yourself fulfilling the good thing that you have submitted. Your mind and body will move in that direction if you persist over a long period of time. Put life's forces to work for you. Think on it, pray for it, believe it—and realize it.

"I am not going to make the decision for you as to what you should be. Only you can do that. I have tried to help by showing you some good patterns to follow. I have tried to help by telling you how you can help yourself once you make your choices.

"In the end, we are all in this game together. We are all teammates and we are all striving to win. With God's help and our own believing efforts, we will."

As Dyer's class concluded and he stepped from the classroom into the sanctuary for worship to begin, the minister realized that news of his resignation speech that was to come later this morning must have leaked out somehow. In the two front pews sat almost every member of the basketball team, with Ramsbottom alongside them. The sorrowful team, disappointed that their investigations had been fruitless, wanted to be present en masse today just to show Dyer their continued gratitude and support.

Just as the opening hymn began, Billy entered the church, the last member of the Tigers to arrive. By his side was Sally, who had at the last minute accepted Billy's invitation to "give church a try just one more time and see."

Just before the message, Reverend Lancaster asked for prayers for Mrs. Hanna, the Trimble Spanish teacher who had been a member at Union many years ago. Her husband had died the previous night, after a two-year bout with cancer. The students would always regret their mistreatment of Mrs. Hanna early in the year, before they became aware of her personal problems. But they were glad that the last few months had been different and that they had been able to be on good terms with her, perhaps making things easier during her husband's last days.

Lancaster preached a short sermon on "love," which Dyer found very comforting. Then, when the hymn of invitation was given, Freddie, Beck, and Billy came forward to confess their belief. Seeing this familiar trio walking down the aisle caused Dyer's heart to leap for joy and made him feel that all his efforts had been worthwhile. This made a total of twelve new members in the past two Sundays. The people were excited to feel the church moving once again. Dyer felt at peace knowing that he had been part of this time of growth at Union. Watching the three basketball players shaking Lancaster's hand gave Dyer a brief bout of sadness, as he realized that he would not be around to watch these three much-loved young people mature in the faith. But the twinge of hesitation did not last for long. Dyer had a job to do, and he was ready to get on with it.

Just as the choral leader motioned for the congregation to sing the final hymn for dismissal, Dyer stepped between the two pulpits, raised his hands and asked for attention. The faces of the congregation, full of smiles as Freddie, Beck, and Billy came forward to confess their faith, suddenly reflected looks of surprise. Dyer proceeded with his announcement by saying, "Dear friends, if I may speak with you a moment. . . ."

Before he could finish his sentence, Clinton Upton advanced swiftly up the platform steps and moved purposefully in front of Dyer, announcing, "Yes, your attention, please. I have something I need to say to everyone here."

As a curious quiet settled over the group, Upton continued, "I have made a mistake of good intention and I must ask forgiveness of everyone—the congregation and especially John Dyer. Over the past few months, I had come to believe that John Dyer was the wrong person to be guiding our youth in this church. I thought that the way he dressed, the motorcycle he drove, and the excessive amount of time he spent with the basketball team were actually bringing harm to our young people. I was also envious of John Dyer because he could get up before a group and speak with such ease, something that I've always struggled to do. I decided that in order to protect our young people—and to make myself feel better too, I guess—I would do something to make John Dyer look bad— so bad that he would have to leave the church.

"I did not steal money from the church, but I did hide four hundred dollars from the collection last week, hoping that it would look as though John took it. I planned to return the money weekly for the next four weeks in the offering plate along with my regular contribution, so that the church would not be hurt. I know now this was wrong, but I thought at the time it was right.

"John Dyer was going to stand up and resign just now because he feared that no one would ever have full confidence in him again. I could not let him do that. You may be wondering how in the world I can get up here and speak after all those years of not being able to say five words in public, of not even being able to teach a Sunday school class because I had such stage fright. To tell the truth, it's the first time I realized that it is easy to speak if you have something to say about what you really believe in. Maybe I have believed *against* things too much of my life, instead of believing *in* them. I guess I simply didn't realize what is really important to me. There are truly meaningful and positive things to say. Again, I am sorry, but I can see a new day ahead for us all. Please say nothing, John Dyer. Just sit down and stay with us."

There were a lot of joyful tears in Union Church that day. It took an hour to get everyone out of the building so that Clinton Upton could close the doors and go home.

As John received his last slaps on the back and embraces from gladdened church members, he walked to the parking lot to find Elmer Mundy and a couple of the other deacons standing near his motorcycle, which was parked alongside Beck's new one. Mundy was patting the leather seat and looking it over as though it was the first time he had laid eyes on a cycle in his life.

"That's a fine machine you've got there, John," Mundy remarked as Dyer approached the group. "Say, would you consider coming to the men's meeting next week and telling everyone the story of your life just like you told the folks in the board meeting last week? It was a very moving tale, and I'd like everyone to hear about how you came to be in the ministry and how you came to have your motorcycle."

Dyer chuckled a little, then reached out and gave Mundy's hand a firm shake. "Mr. Mundy, you have yourself a deal," he said.

As the men walked away to their cars and Dyer revved up his engine to leave the parking lot, he thought to himself that he would always remember this day for many reasons, but mainly as the day that his motorcycle got back in good standing.

In fact, it occurred to him that now even Lucy might approve.

(Below is a copy of John Dyer's cards. Try it yourself for any goals you wish to attain.)

Today Will Be a Great Day

1. Write your goal here— Team—
   Personal—
2. Close your eyes and form the screen. Visualize yourself and your team achieving the success you want.
3. Visualize yourself practicing and playing just as you want.
4. Believe that you are improving in all the things you want to do.

DO THIS MORNING AND NIGHT EVERY DAY

In order to meet our goal
I WILL:

1. Be as encouraging to my teammates as I can be. I will give praise for things well done—even to my teammate who is in competition with me for the same position;
2. Be as enthusiastic about what we are doing as I can be. I will look forward to practices and games;
3. Give my best efforts each day to be the best I can be that day;
4. Regard my teammates as brothers.